SPREADING FIRES

RANDOM HOUSE   NEW YORK

SPREADING
FIRES

BY

JOHN
KNOWLES

Library of Congress Cataloging in Publication Data

Knowles, John, 1926–
  Spreading fires.

  I. Title.
PZ4.K745Sp [PS3561.N68] 813'.5'4 73–5038
ISBN 0–394–46915–1

Manufactured in the United States of America

98765432

First Edition

To T.
The Wizard of Wainscott

SPREADING FIRES

CHAPTER ONE

NEVILLE came with the house. Like it, he was very satisfactory on the surface. Later Brendan Lucas reflected that had he been a more guarded person this surface satisfactoriness itself would have made him wary. Why was an elegant villa on a hillside overlooking Cannes not more expensive? Why was such an ideal cook-servant so readily available?

But he was not guarded. He thought that perhaps he would have done better in many ways, in the Foreign Service for example, if he had been. At age twenty-nine, he had a respectable career in posts around the Middle East behind him, and more such posts ahead. He was the third Brendan Lucas to be in the Foreign Service: an uncle and a grandfather had preceded him.

That summer Brendan had two months' leave. He went back to the States for a short visit and then rented a house near where he had spent so much of his youth, in the South of France.

The house had a name—Mas Tranquilitat, which in the old Provençal language they used to speak there meant simply Tranquillity House. It was built of pale yellow and light brown native stone, with two principal stories plus a large, unused basement and attic. There were long green wooden shutters beside all the big windows. A stone tower terminated the house on the west, and there was a big stone terrace across the front of it, fringed with geraniums. Below the terrace was a sloping grove of orange trees, and then, beyond the gates of the property, the ground continued to fall across descending hills to the sprawl of Cannes and the Mediterranean Sea.

It all sounded beautiful when he rented it sight unseen, and it looked beautiful when he first saw it.

Neville was a stocky, medium-height man a few years older than Brendan, with longish dark blond hair, wearing the conventional black pants and white shirt of a houseman. The first odd thing about him was his nationality: he said he was a Canadian, a Canadian cook making a career of preparing food in, of all places, France. He was not French Canadian, as he took pains to make clear immediately; he was first-generation one-hundred-percent British Canadian and, he tacitly added, proud of it.

For the first few days Neville and Brendan were in this big house alone, the cook clipping across the tile floors to serve Brendan at table, and Zinka, the maid, slopping barefoot behind the scenes with her mop. She said she was Yugoslavian.

At midnight as Brendan went up to bed the third night there, he glimpsed Neville in the kitchen—his kitchen, for already Brendan knew he was that kind of super-possessive cook—preparing a sauce to simmer through the night. His kitchen was never completely still, never entirely cleared. Unlike those mortuary slabs, American kitchens, his quietly throbbed night and day, like the engine of a ship.

The house was Provençal, truly a residence of the South of France, and therefore the kitchen was inevitably its most important room. Kitchens in this part of the world were the basic source of life. Rather religious-minded as he was, Brendan sensed an almost sacramental purpose in them, a consecration here of the staff of life, our daily bread.

The floor of this kitchen was of green and pale yellow tile in floral patterns. Wooden chopping blocks along the wall flanked a large zinc sink, and above, a big window opened on flowering mimosa and the ascending ranks of orange trees.

There was a capacious gas cooking range, great cupboards filled with every kind of pot and sieve and shredder and scraper and casserole, an oval oak kitchen table in the center, a small grate in a corner for a log fire on chilly winter days. The bright, airy room smelled faintly of garlic and oranges and fish. All the worn edges of counters and table attested to decades of tireless work; the real French, the hardworking French, had toiled assiduously here daily, and the big room reflected it.

The one really contemporary note in the kitchen was the wall telephone next to the pantry door. It was the only telephone in this big house. The land-

lord, Brendan reflected, must be authentically and
frugally French.

"You still working?" Brendan said. "Go to bed."

"Nothing better to do, Monsieur Lucas," Neville
replied in his quiet voice, smiling sideways.

"Well, good night."

Next morning, eight-thirty sharp, Neville was in
Brendan's bedroom carrying the breakfast tray,
white napkin, single flower, jam. He put it on the
balcony adjoining the bedroom, built into the tower;
from here there was an exhilarating morning
panorama of the great bowl of hills surrounding
Cannes and of the distant sea.

Later that morning Zinka quit. She could speak no
English, and very little French, so her reasons for
quitting were obscure to Brendan.

She was gone, leaving five bedrooms, a dining
room, big living room, library, and grounds to be
cared for by somebody. Brendan's years of service in
the Middle East meant that he had not lifted a finger
to serve himself in all that time. Who was going to
take care of this place?

"I'll manage, monsieur," said Neville quietly.

"It's all right now, maybe," Brendan objected.
"But when there are five or six houseguests here?"

"I'll manage." Something about his fortitude con-
vinced Brendan that he could. Stiff upper lip. Neville
was a very British kind of Canadian.

Around noon Brendan was sitting on his balcony
reading *Nice-Matin* when Neville appeared.

"Monsieur?"

Brendan looked up from the newspaper.

"I'm so sorry to disturb you, but the shops in the

village will all close in half an hour and I need some supplies. It'll be a big order. I won't be able to carry it. No delivery service in these . . . Mediterranean countries." The last words were said with the quiet distaste of the truly insular Briton.

But these prejudices weren't any of his concern, Brendan thought. "Take the car."

Neville looked shyly at the floor. "I'm so sorry, monsieur. I can't drive. Used to. Had an accident years ago."

That was a disappointment, the very first this ideal servant had caused. "All right," Brendan said with a sigh, such as diplomats use to convey such an emotion without uttering a cross or tactless word. He recognized that diplomats were actors at bottom. Honest men sent abroad to lie for their country was the classic definition of them; his own private one was men of few convictions sent abroad to lose those.

At the village he parked the car near the fountain in the square, and he and Neville crept along the few narrow streets in the heat, from bakery—all the bread was gone—to grocer, wine shop and butcher.

They went in through the red, white and green plastic strips hanging in the doorway. The butcher and his two assistants were just putting the display meat back in the refrigerator while they closed for the two-hour lunch period. With some difficulty they were persuaded to hesitate while Neville made his selection. He was coming between Frenchmen and their meal, always a perilous position to be in. The slight antagonism thus engendered acted on Neville like some terrible affront. His dull green eyes became hooded, his chin went up, jaw locked, and

through unmoving lips he said with the most Angli-
cized French accent Brendan had ever heard that he
wanted a two-kilo leg of lamb. How they understood
his words Brendan couldn't imagine, until he recalled that Neville had come with the house and
must have shopped here very often before. They
procured the leg of lamb. There were other meat
purchases Neville had planned but instead he
turned, indicating with a head gesture that Brendan
should go first, and they went out through the plastic
strips into the breathless noontime-in-July sunshine.

"Bastards!" he said in a combined hiss and groan,
from his depths. His anger seemed extraordinarily
excessive for this little irritation. But he had been
shopping here a long time; perhaps it had been building up.

Back in the car as Brendan drove along the steep
little roads Neville was very nervous, carefully pointing out the menace of a corner, every blind curve.
"It's much shorter on foot," he murmured. "Just
down below your property there's a path leads to a
big drainage pipe, always dry in there, you can walk
through it and come out nearly in the village." He
was silent; then: "Of course, it's quite dangerous in its
way, too."

"How is it dangerous? In what way?"

"Oh well, monsieur . . ." He flung up a hand, indicating he would spare Brendan's gentlemanly sen-
sibilities.

They arrived back at the Mas. It was snoozing in
the high-noon dazzle among its orange trees, subdued, serene—the inexpressible peace of the Mediterranean summer, immemorially calm and unchangeable.

Inside, the shutters facing south had been closed by Neville before they set out, and the house with its big, high-ceilinged rooms and tile floors remained cool. The furniture consisted of a few good period pieces every French household had to have—a big wooden cupboard, a side table, a settee—and some French manufacturer's idea of furniture for Palm Beach: deep white chairs, iron and glass tables, low-slung couches.

The library alone was undilutedly French. The desk was a creaking old affair of many small drawers and sliding panels, the chairs were Louis XV, the walls were lined with leather-bound French classics, there were gray-and-white prints of mythological hunting scenes, a music stand and next to it an old violin in a glass case. An ancient, brocaded, straight-backed couch stood against one wall. Hanging from the top of a bookcase there was a nearly disintegrated heraldic banner. The room smelled of confined old pages in ancient books. The small shaded lamps gave off a yellowish, period glow.

Behind the desk was a window divided into two big panes opening inward, and beyond was a heavy iron grille with two stout shutters on the outside. In fact, the villa was girded for attack on all fronts. Every exterior door was massive, windowless, and powerfully double-locked. All the windows had these heavy shutters and all of them on the ground floor were grilled as well.

Brendan had lunch at a little umbrella table on the stone terrace overlooking Cannes and the sea. It was quite hot there, but Neville had indicated that this was where the lunch he had prepared should properly be eaten and to help him regain his calm after the butcher incident Brendan went along with it. Lunch was tomatoes Provençal, Dover sole, wild rice, and the Italian dessert custard *zabaglione.* It was very good in an odd way. To pin a national label on Neville's cooking was impossible: "Oh, monsieur, I've traveled everywhere. I pick up my recipes along the way. Can't go home, you see."

Brendan swam at the beach in Cannes that afternoon, had dinner at the Carlton, took in a couple of jammed night clubs and arrived back at the Mas very late. Seeing a light in the kitchen (Neville was of all things still working at this hour), he decided to go in that way. He knocked at the kitchen door. In a frozen voice Neville cried, "Go away! Who is it?"

"It's me, the boss!"

"Speak again! I can't hear you!"

That was a lie. Nevertheless Brendan yelled, "It's me, Brendan Lucas! I live here!" He understood that Neville needed to hear him speak more words in order to be absolutely certain it was indeed Brendan and not some super-clever impersonator. He was beginning to understand Neville.

There was the sound of a key turning, followed by a bolt being drawn, and then Neville cautiously opened the kitchen door, admitted him, glanced around outside and relocked the door.

"Why are you working so late again? It's not necessary."

Neville returned to the ironing board and resumed work on a shirt of Brendan's. "It helps me when I'm nervous," he eventually answered. The incident at the butcher shop apparently still had him thoroughly upset. The iron slapped rhythmically down on the shirt. "It helps my nerves. It's something, Monsieur Lucas, being an exile."

"Yes, I'll bet it is. I'm an exile, too, in a way. But if it bothers you why don't you go home, at least for a visit?"

"Can't do that. Can't go home. They . . ."

"Yes?"

"Well, you know Canada."

"I don't really."

"Well, monsieur, it's not like the States, I suppose. Big corporations control it all. And the Crown, British Crown. Princess Marina of Kent and those. They would get control of me if I went back."

"What? How?"

Hesitating, Neville sighed and finally said, "I have some property, a house in Toronto, I'm heir to it, it's my stepfather's, and they want it, they want to get control of it. You see, I used to be a nurse, male nurse, in the service, and what happens is they get you to work on a case and they pretend you blundered and ruined somebody's health, pretending you gave some patient the wrong medicine and so he had a heart attack, a stroke, maybe he died, and they pretend you're responsible and they'll hush it up only if you agree to do their bidding. And their bidding makes you maybe commit a *real* crime, you have to, to protect yourself, and then they've really got you. Then they make me turn over the house in Toronto to them. That's what they want to do if I go back."

Well, Brendan assuredly did not know Canada if that was the way it was.

The next day, Sunday, as a reasonably good Catholic, Brendan went to Mass in the little church in the village. In the world of diplomacy, with its matter-of-fact deceptions and lies and betrayals and cynicism, he felt he would have risked complete demoralization without this adherence to a God of love.

The church was ancient and tiny and dark. The main door, a huge piece of wood dried and splintered, with corroded bolts and hinges, was as old as France. As he passed into the interior it was so dark that only the voices reciting the responses of the Mass showed that he was not alone with the priest and the altar boy. Effigies of the Virgin and the saints stood in the gloom above flickering votary lamps. The Mass proceeded, all was calm and all was dark; perhaps his life was being blessed.

Going out afterward he saw to his great surprise Neville lingering at a side altar. There was a painting of St. Sebastian above it, with all the arrows piercing his body visible in the dimness. Neville turned as he passed him, and it went through Brendan's mind that this was a rehearsed, not a chance encounter.

"I didn't know you were a Catholic, Neville." He seemed so English, Brendan would have thought Episcopalian, or Anglican, or whatever it was called in Canada.

"I believe in the old things, monsieur." Neville was holding a thick, worn missal tightly in his left hand. "This is the true old church, isn't it?"

"Well, *I* think so . . ."

They started down the little cobblestone street toward the village square. Neville was dressed in his go-to-church best: navy blue suit, tightly buttoned, a white shirt, maroon tie. He made a rather impressive appearance dressed formally in this way. Only his colorless face detracted from it.

The homeless of France—that is, the Algerian workmen who had come there—loitered along the street, nothing to do on a workless Sunday, not even go to the mosque. Truly fish out of water, they stood and stared and waited.

"Vermin," muttered Neville.

Brendan paced beside him for a short distance. Putting up with Neville's prejudices was becoming a bore. He started to make some sharp rejoinder, and then, perhaps by diplomatic reflex, settled for a truism: "There are good and bad Algerians, just as there are in every other group."

They moved along, Neville in a moody silence. Then he said, "You don't know them."

"I've lived among the Arabs for years. I *do* know them. Some are good and some are bad, but most are mixtures. Just like English Canadians."

Neville drew in his breath sharply, as though he had been unexpectedly jabbed with a needle. Maybe Brendan shouldn't have brought the point home that directly. Neville's feelings were so strong, and so deeply interred, that it was impossible to gauge them. Brendan began to see why he was such a solitary. Being with people would be painful for him. And, from the point of view of others, he was not good company.

They reached the village square. There was a circular granite fountain in the middle, a pedestal holding a bronze statue of a classical youth, water dripping from the pedestal into the surrounding pool. The terraces of the two cafés were full of people, out for their Sunday airing. No one spoke to Neville; he spoke to no one.

"How long did you say you've been working here?" Brendan asked casually.

"Three years."

His extreme solitude and ceaseless work were beginning to trouble Brendan. A Jordanian peasant would complain at such hours.

But he seemed content. He often hummed, tonelessly to be sure, at his work, and his continual movements about the house and through the orange grove were those of a contentedly busy person doing fulfilling work. He took several opportunities to say how much he enjoyed working for Brendan, broadly hinting that he would like to be with him wherever he was stationed. Brendan was not sure moving a Canadian with him from place to place would be convenient or even possible. But he began to think about it.

Neville spent these days almost entirely in the kitchen. Brendan, as the date when the first of his guests would arrive drew closer, tried to spend some time there with him while he still could. Once Mimi and Xavier arrived, and then Ariane and his mother, everything at the Mas Tranquilitat would alter, quicken, and the whole point of the house and summer begin to unfold.

Neville the Canadian was in the kitchen a fully worthy successor to the assiduous French who had preceded him there. As he moved from counter to table to cupboard in his black and white garb there was an almost ritualistic calm and formality to his movements, an almost symbolic significance, fulfilling the age-old formulas dictated by the room.

"You really are cut off here, aren't you?" Brendan began on a visit to the kitchen one day.

"Oh." A shrug. He went on polishing Brendan's shoes.

"You haven't had a day off to see your friends. When do you want one, or two?"

"We'll see, we'll see, so much to do . . ."

"Well, at least you won't have to spend so much time alone once my sister Mimi arrives—"

Neville's hand paused on the shoes. Then it continued.

Looking quizzically at him, uncomprehending, Brendan went on, "She won't be able to stay very long." The polishing grew firmer. "She's quite a good ballerina, pretty well known in that field, and being that takes the dedication of a nun. Some of them get married, but . . . I don't know . . ." Why was he going into intimacies with him? Next he would begin telling him all that was dangerously wrong with Xavier, his "best friend" to whom he'd introduced his sister and whom she was now determined to marry. They had *both* been alone too much.

"Yes?" Neville looked up with interest, something he rarely betrayed. His usual demeanor was one of passive indifference. "I know how that is, with these ladies of the theater."

"Oh, well . . ." Having gone this far, Brendan had to defend her. "She's been at it since she was three or something, and she's not a 'lady of the theater' in the sense I think you mean it, not like a . . . chorus girl or anything like that *at all*. First of all she's a soloist, a star, a prima ballerina, she studied with Danilova herself, and she's—Miriam's—well, distinguished." That ended his discussion of Mimi's character. He went back to the point he had started to make. "She'll want to spend a lot of time with you in the kitchen. She *loves* cooking. I don't mean she'll interfere, she'll just want to keep you company, learn from you. Help you with the shopping. You'll have some company, once Miriam is here."

"I don't mind," Neville said. Brendan didn't stop to wonder what that meant. "I'll go to the village soon as I've finished polishing your boots," he added. Brendan had never asked or expected him to take care of his shoes, but he had decided to give up attempting to limit his toil.

"Do I need to take you in the car?"

"Oh no, monsieur, that won't be necessary. Just a small order I can carry back through the lower path. I'll just take my stick along with me." He indicated a formidable club in the corner. It was like an American baseball bat except longer and thicker.

"What's that for?"

He polished away for several moments and then said quietly, "There's Arabs hang around that path, around that drainage pipe. They'll jump you if they dare. They won't dare with me carrying my stick."

"How many times has that happened to anyone along that path?"

He made no answer but went on polishing busily. Then he said, "You don't see many hippies and that lot hanging around Cannes these days, do you?"

Brendan had to admit he didn't. "I guess it's too expensive for them."

Neville went on polishing, but there was a sardonic half-smile on his wide face. "You have been in the

Holy Land and remote places like that, monsieur. You don't know what's happening. But I've been here. I know. The French police are very severe police. They see hippies and they arrest them. Then late at night when no one can see or hear they take them back there . . ." He cocked his head toward the bigger interior hills and added in a muffled, lifeless tone, "And then they shoot them. I don't sleep some- times. So I've heard it. I'm the only one has."

The next day Neville asked Brendan to drive him down to the open-air market in Cannes. "With your . . . sister . . . arriving I'll have to lay in some more supplies." He said the word "sister" with a peculiar intonation, the way he might pronounce the name of some very singular religion to which Brendan ad- hered. "And are there to be other guests, monsieur?"

"Yes, an old friend of mine, Xavier Farel de Dor- nay. Very fancy name, isn't it?"

"He must be a nobleman."

"Xavier's a stockbroker in Paris. I think his family did have a title in the old days."

"If your blood is noble, then it is always noble. Unless you marry into the wrong class. Then your children lose it. Has he married into the wrong class?"

"Uh, not yet."

They walked down through the shimmering orange grove, through the gate and got into the car. "I understood there was to be more than just two guests, monsieur. Not meaning to pry."

"There's my mother, Miriam's and my mother, she's coming. And Xavier's sister is coming. It's a family party." Well, why not make it clear, for God's sake. "You see, Miriam wants to marry Xavier, plans to marry him. So there is a . . . prenuptial house party, so to speak."

Brendan had said "wants to marry," not "is engaged to." Both were true, but the second seemed much more binding. Miriam bound to Xavier? Sometimes that made her seem to Brendan like the heroine of an old movie, lashed to the tracks in the path of the oncoming express. At other times . . . well, Xavier *was* capable of sincere devotion.

And Brendan had haphazardly, without dreaming of any consequences, introduced her to one of the best-looking and most charming fourflushers in France—or, if not a fourflusher nor cad nor scoundrel nor wastrel nor any of those other figures out of nineteenth-century melodrama, then an unstable man, twentieth-century style.

"This curve here, monsieur," Neville said hesitantly. Brendan braked a little. They turned into the Boulevard Carnot, which descended through its flanking rows of plane trees to Cannes.

The market was held in a great rust-colored open-air pavilion. Brendan drove up the ramp attached to it and parked on the roof, on a level with the attics of Old Cannes, open to the beneficent blue sun-suffused sky.

Below, on the floor of the market, all was cheerful bustle. These people here were for the most part the true Provençals, that talented, talkative, joking and slightly wacky race which inhabit this Mediterranean enclave and have done practically always.

"Brendan!" called a cordial French voice behind him. "What are you selling here in the market, eh?"

It was Pierre Vervier, proprietor and chef of a converted mill where the Lucases used to dine when they lived in Nice. "Me?" Brendan replied. "I'm selling American military secrets. Want any?"

That was the right irreverent Provençal note. Pierre laughed. Big and boisterous, owner of one of the best restaurants here, he was a celebrity in the Cannes market. "You don't know anything about food," he exclaimed, clapping a hand on Brendan's shoulder. "Why are you here really? To steal?"

"Steal? This crap here? If I want to steal I go to the supermarket, where all the really good things are in plastic."

"Of course. Naturally. Soon you'll be plastic too, brain and all. And who is this gentleman?" he went on cordially, turning toward Neville.

"This is Monsieur Neville . . ." Brendan didn't even know his last name. "He's working with me this summer." Brendan immediately realized it was phony American egalitarianism to say "with" instead of "for."

"I am Monsieur Lucas's cook and housekeeper," said Neville with quiet dignity. Brendan had been put in his place, like it or not. In Neville's European-ized universe everyone had his assigned place in the hierarchy and was proud of it. Brendan felt that his own head, full of the sloppy American stew that everybody was all just folks together, was a lie Neville wouldn't support.

"And now"—Pierre clapped his hands in anticipation—"to work." As they strolled through the market Brendan explained Neville's background very briefly to him. "You hire an English Canadian to cook for

you *here!* You *are* mad! Ah, Mireille," he said to a
buxom, black-haired beauty poised among vegetable
crates, "show me some good lettuce. And I don't
mean these lousy heads here, which are fit only for
rabbits."

"And this one!" she cried passionately, seizing a
head of lettuce from another crate. "Is that fit only
for rabbits! Look at it! It's beautiful! It's crying, 'Eat
me, eat me!' "

Pierre gazed with lids humorously half-closed at
her and murmured, "Later," then sauntered on.
They passed crates of grapes and peaches, piles of
cucumbers and peppers and fresh eggs. Fat ladies in
blue smocks sat knitting next to their weighing
scales. There was a low wooden table of herbs—basil,
thyme, lavender, oregano, sage, rosemary, garlic,
marjoram, *rhomarria, camamila, foil, vervens.*
There were melons, cabbages, radishes, onions,
mushrooms. There was an open counter displaying
hams and salami and pâté, skinned and gutted rabbits, dressed chickens. There was a bank of delecta-
ble cheeses, and next to it a long parade of cut flowers.

They drifted out of this shed and toward the shops
which bordered it. Pierre stopped at a fish stall—sole,
rouget, daurade, tuna, oysters, mussels, clams, crabs,
shrimp—and the owner invited them into the tiny
bar next-door to talk over things in general with a
glass of good, strong Pernod. Eleven A.M.: about time
to start drinking. This was France.

Brendan remembered Neville, and looked around.
He was standing still on the sidewalk outside, clutch-
ing a fish he had bought wrapped in a newspaper.

Brendan signaled to him to come in. He shook his head and moved off a step or two to examine some clams.

"You know something," said the fishmonger. "If Mireille wears that dress any lower I'm going to take her into the dairy one day and milk her."

"I thought you had already," remarked Pierre.

"And you?"

"Me? I'm too old for milkmaids, you know that."

"The day you're too old they'll have you laid out in Our Lady of Hope up there on the hill singing the Requiem over you."

"It's possible," admitted Pierre quietly.

"And you, *mon potte*, who are you?"

Brendan explained who he was.

"Why do you speak French so well?"

"Because I listen." That answer was pure reflex; Brendan let it stand. Besides, it was true.

"You do listen, that can be seen. It's rare among young people today."

"I'm not so young. Twenty-nine."

"That's young. Maybe *you* should milk Mireille."

"De Gaulle wouldn't want an *American* using that national treasure."

The fishmonger laughed abruptly and eyed him. Not only did he speak French, he had a Provençal turn of mind.

"Monsieur," said Neville sibilantly from the doorway of the bar. "Can I speak to you a moment? So sorry to interrupt."

Useless to ask Neville to come and say what he wanted in front of the others, although it would surely be no more confidential than asking whether

Brendan wanted more rosé or red wine for the cellar.

"Monsieur," he continued with quiet urgency on the sidewalk, "do you think we should get some pâté or some salami for lunch tomorrow?"

"Both."

"Both?"

"Yes. Lots of both." Brendan went back to join Pierre and the fishmonger, annoyed without really knowing why. Neville was only doing his job. Still Brendan was vexed. Maybe it was just having to work with someone so completely un-Provençal in Provençe. Brendan loved Provençe. Provençe was a part of him. Neville, and all he stood for, were alien.

A little later, after buying his round of Pernod, he left the bar and started back toward the car through all the bustle, all the abundance of the marketplace. The French streak in him suddenly rejoiced in all it saw and smelled here. When he had first come to France in his teens, there was a gray hangover from the war still visible—gray and hungry and threadbare postwar France. And now here she was as she was meant to be: possessing really everything.

He wandered in a quiet euphoria—half in love with France and one-quarter drunk—up the ramp to the car parked among the rooftops.

Neville was sitting in it with the supplies he had bought. These included a large metal drum.

"What's that?"

"Kerosene," he answered. "Sometimes the electricity gets cut off, up at the Mas. I like to have kerosene lamps ready and waiting."

Brendan had to give him credit for thinking of everything. "My friend Pierre there seems to be buddies with everyone in the market," he remarked.

After a brooding silence Neville said with nasal distaste, "He gets a kickback from them on everything he buys there, he gets a cut on everything under the table. That's why they're all so friendly. You know. Thick as thieves."

CHAPTER
TWO

BRENDAN met Miriam at two in the afternoon at Nice Airport. She was wearing an orange pants suit and had an orange scarf over her head, and huge dark glasses hiding her eyes. Her tanned feet were pushed into wooden wedge shoes. Miriam was not one to pass unnoticed.

They got her bags and set off in the car. "It's weird coming back here. Like having a dream about your childhood."

"I love coming here," Brendan said.

"I know you do. You're in love with your own past. That's why you're not married yet."

"That's not the reason."

"Isn't it?"

Brendan turned into the Autoroute which sliced through the hills behind the coast.

"I'm not going to be left sitting around like you," she went on. "Xavier—"

"The perfect husband" popped out of him, as though they were bickering teenagers again.

"He may not be perfect, but he *is* a man!"

That was certainly true.

"And I *am* a woman!"

And that!

"I hope you'll be deliriously happy together." Somehow Brendan could not escape his sarcastic-adolescent tone.

"You sound so funny. And about your best friend, too."

"Best friend and brother-in-law are two different things."

She took off her dark glasses to study his face. "I'm not sure you want me to marry *anyone.*" She went on studying him. "That's very Irish of you. The Irish secretly want a world full of spinsters and bachelors. And they've pretty well got it in their own country."

"That's crazy. Of course I want you to get married —married . . . when it's going to make you happy."

"Yes, you do, you do." She paused. "And you don't."

They drove on in silence. Out of the corner of his eye when her head was partially turned the other way he looked her over. She was, of course, exquisite.

Even then he knew what jealousy was. Jealousy was an expression of inadequacy: people are envious because they are deeply frightened, frightened that they don't possess enough to survive by themselves, to flourish with no one to lean on.

They arrived at the Mas. He honked for Neville to come and help with the bags. Neville did not appear. He blasted the horn. No response.

"Let's go up to the house. We'll leave the bags. He must be in the basement or somewhere."

The front door was open. They went in and through the living room and dining room and pantry to the kitchen. Neville was peeling something at the sink. "Didn't you hear me honking? There are some bags to bring in."

He turned, wiping his hands on his white waist apron. "I'm sorry. I didn't know that was you, monsieur. So many noises hereabouts sometimes."

The house and grounds stood alone surrounded by pine woods: silent.

"This is my sister. This is Neville."

"How d'you do, miss," he said very quietly.

"Hello, Neville. Denny's told me what a wonderful cook you are." She looked around. The quiet, steady undercurrent of continuous preparation flowed noticeably along. "You can tell good food is prepared in this kitchen. It's the atmosphere here, the way it looks, the way it smells. I wouldn't be surprised if even *I* could fix a decent meal here."

Neville had some kind of tiny momentary reflex, indecipherable, then said, "I'll just go see about your luggage," and went out the kitchen door.

Brendan took Miriam upstairs. His bedroom, the master bedroom next to the tower, opened on a large white bathroom, and on the other side of that was a smaller but still large bedroom, with a door to some outside stairs descending to the front terrace. It was the only bedroom beside his which was large enough for two people to use. "When is Xavier getting here?" she asked casually. "He wasn't sure in his last letter."

"I heard from him yesterday. Not until early next week. He has to go to Vichy with his mother while she has her liver purged or something like that."

"French people and their livers," she said irritably. "His mother . . . Vichy . . ." She began to comb her hair very firmly.

"Don't you like your future mother-in-law?"

"Shut up." She went on combing, and then said airily, "Which of these beds do you think he'll want? I mean, you're a man, which one would, uh, you think he'd want?"

The one *you're* in, he wanted to yell at her. "Gosh, I don't know," he said. Brendan hadn't used the word "gosh" since he was about seventeen years old.

They had both been brought up strict Catholics. And the seemingly casual way she and Xavier had simply begun a sexual life together complete with everything except a ceremony and children profoundly jarred something in Brendan. No one else's doing so would have affected him at all. He had done so himself more than once. It was, as they say, done these days, even by people brought up strict Catholics. But it was not supposed to be done by Miriam, not before him. It loosened something elemental and dangerous.

The hell with it. This was July, this was the South of France, they were young and they even had a certain amount of money. The weather was wonderful and would continue to be wonderful. And, to take

care of the nuts and bolts of their lives, they had
Neville.

They spent a number of tranquil days around the
house as July gave way to August.

"Mimi!" Brendan called from his bedroom to her
through the bathroom one morning. "Get suited up.
We're going—"

"Get *what?*"

"Suited up."

"Oh. I thought you said 'sweated up.' It sounded
like ballet class for a minute. What does 'suited up'
mean?"

"Put on your bathing suit. I'm taking you to the
sea."

"Now that's what I call good thinking."

And they drove down to the sea. Never mind that
there were five times too many people there in July,
and would be twenty times too many in August. The
sea was the sea.

Brendan Lucas had always felt powerfully drawn
to the sea. For many years he never understood why.
He had been born and brought up in Washington,
D.C., well inland from the Atlantic Ocean, and there
was no family connection of any kind with seagoing
life.

It was true that several summers during his boy-
hood Brendan's parents rented houses at one or another Atlantic beach, and he supposed it was at the
first of these—at Rehoboth Beach, Delaware—that
his obsession, his inebriated devotion to the sea began.

Can the sand have been as white, as satiny as he

remembered it? Can the beach have been as vast, the shelter under the boardwalk as coolly mysterious, the edge of the sea as frothy with vigorous life, the sky as limitless and exuberant with sea gulls as he remembered it? He was seven or eight and he lived those weeks in an ecstasy of world marvels, all the artifacts and crosscurrents and fringe treasures and above all the transporting immortal sea smell of the Atlantic Ocean.

Brendan knew a reef off Cap d'Antibes and they took a speedboat out to it, anchored, and swam in the silvery blue water, shared with many transparent fish who evidenced no fear nor interest in them. If nothing else on the Riviera in July, there was enough sea for all.

They put on face masks and breathing tubes and kick fins, and this simple equipment gave them access to, made them a part of, the underseas, at one with sea horses and sea urchins and mussels and crayfish and stingrays, all those ugly freaks of the sea. They were ugly freaks, too, as sea creatures, no gills, only artificial fins, much too unstreamlined for proper gliding, thrashers. Still they thrashed about energetically, and the cool salty water performed for him, and maybe for her, its baptismal renewal.

Then they drove back to the Mas and dressed, and he took her out around the grounds, through the grove of orange trees.

"They're ugly little buggers, aren't they," she remarked, picking an orange. He hadn't noticed; he took a look at them. The oranges were small and gnarled, tough. They looked very sour, inedible. These trees seemed to be a recessive strain, decadent, incapable of producing anything edible.

"What are those little bags?" she asked, pointing to tiny whitish sacks which hung at many points on all of the trees.

"I've been meaning to ask Neville," he said. "Some kind of protection against bugs, I guess."

"Yes," replied Neville when asked as he passed them a few minutes later on his way to the gate, "that's what they're for. To keep the insects from attacking the trees."

"What's in the sacks?" asked Miriam.

"Arsenic, miss," Neville replied quietly.

"Goodness," she said in mock shock, but not quite mock enough. She was shocked; so was Brendan. "Xavier's sure to be bringing his dog with him," she observed.

"That big German shepherd?"

Neville was following the conversation. Brendan suddenly didn't have to be told that Neville was afraid of dogs, especially big dogs, preeminently German shepherds. People with arid childhoods were. And one look at Neville's taut, cheerless, sallow face spoke loudly of an arid childhood—and not much of a fertile life since.

"Well," Brendan said, "those bags of arsenic are going to have to go."

There were hundreds and hundreds of them, tiny grayish sacks, evil-looking, like parasites in their cocoons waiting to creep out and attack the life they infested. Of course the trees themselves were, he now saw, a little repugnant with their stunted trunks, knobby, twisted limbs and hard, inedible fruit.

"Those bags have been there a long time," mur-mured Neville. "I doubt the poison's very effective any more."

"Still," Brendan said, "they could make the dog good and sick, even if they didn't kill him. I want them all removed."

"And besides," added Miriam, "I don't *like* being surrounded by hundreds of bags of arsenic. Do you? And it isn't as though these trees could grow any-thing anyone could eat."

After dinner that night Brendan glimpsed Neville out among the trees, harvesting the poison. "Not to-night, Neville!" he called out to him. "Tomorrow! We'll all do it together."

"Tomorrow could be a busy day," he replied.

The next morning Mimi had breakfast with Bren-dan on his tower balcony, and told him she was going to drive down to Cannes for a ballet class. "Thank God there's one here!" she exclaimed. "I haven't had one in *three days*. Feels like I'm falling apart."

He asked her to spend what time she could with Neville, keeping him company and going shopping with him, because he was so solitary and such a hard-working man. She said she would.

Then Brendan went out among the trees with a big basket and began picking off the poison. Neville was doing the same on the other side of the house. It took hours in the hot sun to gather these tiny bags of old death and get them out of the way.

Miriam returned at one in the afternoon. Neither of them was very hungry, so Brendan asked Neville to give them just some salami and cheese and a loaf

of bread. The food was served on the terrace and
they nibbled at it.

In the afternoon Brendan had some errands to do
in Cannes. Miriam stayed at the Mas.

After he came back he took a shower and a short
nap and then joined her on the terrace for cocktails.
The immemorial dusk of the South of France, a
smoky blue evocation of some sensual eternity, co-
hered shade by shade over the hills around them and
the coast below.

"Let's eat out tonight," suggested Miriam. Neville
was placing a bowl of nuts on the table.

"Good idea," Brendan said. "What about some
bouillabaisse?"

"Or one of the places in Old Cannes. I heard
they're scrumptious."

"There's a little mill—converted mill—near here
with some of the best food in France." Neville had
stepped back into the house. "You remember, Pierre
Vervier's place. We used to go there as kids."

"Of course!"

They decided to go to the mill. After finishing the
drinks Miriam started down through the trees toward the car and Brendan went into the kitchen to
tell Neville. He was beating something in a bowl,
hard. "But monsieur," he remonstrated quietly without looking up, "I have a nice duck here I was going
to prepare, and—"

"It can wait till tomorrow, can't it? Take the evening off, or the night for that matter. Isn't there anybody you'd like to spend the night with?" The sensual air around here was getting into everything
Brendan said.

"Monsieur?" Neville said gravely as Brendan turned to go.

"Yes?"

"Monsieur," he went on evenly, "can you . . . will you kindly keep her out of my kitchen?"

"Her? Keep—you mean my sister?"

He returned to beating rhythmically in the bowl.

"But she's so interested in your work. And I thought you'd enjoy some company."

"It would be better, monsieur, if you don't mind. Keep her out of my kitchen."

Brendan stood there, a little irritated, and then said in an offhand way, "All right."

Good cooks were notoriously temperamental. Usually they drank on the sly too. At least he hadn't been troubled with that.

Joining Mimi in the car Brendan said casually, "Did you learn anything in the kitchen from Neville this afternoon?"

"Yes," she said in her husky voice, "that he *doesn't want visitors!* Goodness. Wouldn't let me help him with a damn thing. And his eyes kind of—I don't know—rolled around in his head in a funny way. Like Petrouchka's. I've seen photos of Nijinksy in that role. Just like that. Loose eyes."

"What's Petrouchka?"

"*Petrouchka.* The ballet about the doll which half comes to life. He looked like that, like a loose doll or something. But I knew you wanted me to keep him company and so I tried and tried. And at last I *did* get him talking, but my God what stories! People getting kidnapped out of villas around here by Al-

gerians and butchered! I wasn't going to tell you, and
then I was, and then—"

"It's all right," Brendan said with a little laugh.
"He's hipped on fantasies like that."

After Mimi and Brendan left for dinner, Neville
stopped working at the sink. He opened a small door
in the kitchen and mounted the dark, narrow back
stairway to the second floor and went along the corridor there to Miriam's room. Entering it he stood
contemplating her cosmetics on the dressing table, a
pair of panty hose tossed at the foot of the bed, a
night robe. His hands opened and shut, opened and
shut. Then he turned and went back to the kitchen.

They dined outdoors at the mill, beside a hurrying
mountain stream. Pierre's pâté was all provocative
flavor, the beef bourguignon was authoritative, there
was a snappy salad and a chocolate soufflé for dessert.

"Now that's what I call a good dinner!" Mimi exclaimed.

"I don't think the food at my place is so bad."

"That's true. And it's cheaper."

"For you," he said grimly, remembering Neville's
astronomical shopping bills. Nothing but the best
would ever do. Brendan was beginning to get sick of
the bills, he realized as he sat replete in his chair at
the mill, and also of so much too good, too elaborate
food at home, day after day. It was almost as though
Neville were trying to prove something to him, as
though he were competing for the Blue Ribbon of
High International Cuisine. Brendan would have to
speak to him, tell him he wanted to eat more plainly.

He knew this would displease the cook very much. He knew Neville cared nothing about the hours he must slave in the kitchen to produce these fancy feasts. They were intended to tell Brendan something. Getting that message through was all that mattered. But Brendan didn't know what the message was, and couldn't be expected to care.

They went on from the mill down into Cannes, to the gambling casino where Miriam proceeded to lose a bundle at baccarat. Brendan played a little roulette and so lost only a little bundle. They sipped champagne steadily, though, and when they left they were poorer and wiser but happier. They drove to a raucous and extremely expensive night club with walls made out of straw, where she taught him the latest country-rock-western dance variations in the middle of the dance floor. Finally they ended by doing the cancan for the customers. That was the kind of effect Miriam had on him.

Driving back to the Mas through the black and deserted country roads of the hills they were still wide awake, so there were more dancing lessons to the record player in the living room. Brendan got out a bottle of champagne—Neville had laid in a dozen bottles of Dom Pérignon and for once the extravagance proved useful—and, physically fatigued at last but mentally stimulated, they settled down to a session of Russian bank. At a very late hour Miriam went to the kitchen, where she made some café au lait and found some rolls. They went out on the terrace and looked down over the gray-black pool of Cannes below.

Night silence on the Mediterranean is not what it

is elsewhere. It is wider and more significant and has more reverberations. It sounds the centuries: some cavernous meaning echoes in its innards, its remembrances.

Gradually from Italy the palest of ivory-blue skies began to float high over the eastern hills and the lights of the coast, which slowly failed before the rising, limitlessly hopeful and intact morning shine spreading over them.

Brendan woke sometime in the middle of the day to hear a swishing noise in the hallway. It sounded like a lady in a long evening train moving slowly up and down the corridor outside his door. He turned over and tried to go back to sleep, but the great lady continued her soft but resolute parading up and down outside the bedroom door.

He got up, crossed and opened the door. Neville, on hands and knees, was scrubbing the floor of the hallway. "Oh, I wondered what it was," Brendan said.

"I'm sorry if I disturbed you. With no meals to fix . . . something useful to do . . ."

"Yes. Right. Will you fix some breakfast for Miss Lucas and me."

"She's dead to the world," said Neville quietly.

"Better make her some anyway."

He got Miriam up and they had breakfast in his tower at three in the afternoon.

For dinner they had Neville's duck; it was very good but after the excesses of the day before Brendan could only pick at it, and Miriam almost completely abstained to make up for yesterday's soufflé

and champagne. They went to bed early, having decided to make an excursion into the interior the next
day.

It was a memorable day. The sky was a dome of
wisest Mediterranean blue, the hills reared up asser-
tively toward the great flanks of the Maritime Alps.
They wound upward to Grasse, then further inland
along mountain roads. Finally they came to the ancient walled town of Gourdon, its ramparts crowning
the top of a sheer cliff below which the country fell
steeply away toward the coast, an impregnable inland fortress of long ago, of the days of Old Provençe,
troubadours, love courts, pirates, robber barons. Miriam was charmed by its tiny streets and staunch stone
houses.

They had a picnic in a steep meadow in the moun-
tains, slices of cheese and salami in sandwiches of
long French bread, and a little red wine. It was like
summer afternoons when they were in their teens,
and used to bicycle together along the back roads of
the Riviera.

They sat beneath a Mediterranean pine, Mimi's
tanned, beautiful legs stretched out in front of her.
Not for her the bunchy, wrestler's muscles in many
ballerina's legs; hers were strong, God knew, but
smooth, sinuous, tapering. He looked at her in her
short, fitted little summer dress. Her small torso and
small breasts, long and graceful arms, long neck and
small, shapely head were designed by nature expressly for the classical ballet. If she hadn't gone into
it voluntarily, George Balanchine would have kidnapped her. And there was that tantalizing suggestion of Spanish about her: while she had the family

blue eyes, her skin had an olive cast instead of the high coloring of her mother and brother, and her features had a certain set to them—high cheekbones, small but firm nose—which distantly and faintly echoed that Spanish seaman who had grafted himself into their ancestry.

"It's funny," he remarked. "When we were kids, you were dedicated to a career and I was in love all the time. Now you're getting married and I'm left with nothing *but* a career, such as it is."

He remembered years before crossing from New York to Le Havre on the *Liberté* with Mimi and his mother. It was in June; the ship was full. Mimi, who was about thirteen, went religiously every day to the little gymnasium with its old-fashioned workout machines to do her ballet exercises. Brendan went along to watch her. He had never seen Mimi dance before. It had never entered his head to accompany her to ballet class, and he had finagled his way out of attending her recitals.

But now, with nothing better to do on the high seas, he liked to watch her long, skinny legs in black tights go tentatively yet already gracefully through the classical positions. She was never out of sorts then. On her face she had a transported look, charmed. Could this grace really be coming from *me*, she seemed to be wondering joyously to herself. Even the light rolling of the great ship failed to interfere with her instinctual balance, and her developing skill.

One day, as he lay sprawled next to the rowing machine grinning up at her, the door swung open and their mother stepped in. "You're not supposed to

be in here now!" she said indignantly to Brendan.
"Watching her practically in her undergarments!
What are you thinking of!"

He had not been aware of thinking of anything
except how nice she looked and how well she moved.
What else would he be thinking of? And then her
rebuke created for the first time in his mind the
shadow of a seminal thought.

Now, as they lounged in the shade of the Mediterranean pine, he kept himself by long-ingrained habit
from more than glancing at her legs or at anything
else about her. She was saying, "I'm not going to give
my dancing up. Not yet for a while. Xavier under-
stands that. He wants me to go on."

"The money from your ballet company is lousy, of
course, but the concertizing pays off pretty well."

"It's not the money!" She glared at him. "It's the
—the *aura* it gives me . . ."

"The *aura!*" He snorted. "Oh, my God!"

"The *aura*. He *loves* my aura."

But Brendan secretly supposed that her being a
ballet star was indeed one of her great fascinations
for Xavier. Deeply buried under the Parisian veneer
was a romantic and wondering boy. It was in that boy
that Brendan placed his hopes for Miriam's happi-
ness. And he did want her to be happy. He wanted
her to be married and he wanted her to be happy.

"You know something," he said to her.

"What?"

"If you—well, if you ever—well, uh . . ."

"If what?"

"If, uh, ever things with you and Xavier didn't
work out—well, you know I'm always—there's al-

ways—wherever I happen to be living you can always come and—"

She touched his mouth with her long fingers. "I'm going to come and see you anyway, wherever you are. You know that." She pulled up some grass and began nibbling it. "And things are going to work out with Xavier. I'm what he needs. I'm strong. I know he isn't, in certain ways. But I am."

Well, of course, she was. She could not have followed through on that grueling career from the age of eight if she hadn't been.

They descended to the coast through the gorge of the Loup River, steep, craggy, crowded with evergreens, a spectacular, narrow swatch which the river had cut between the mountain and the sea. A fine day. They were feeling their best when they drove up to the Mas around six o'clock.

The house looked wrong. First of all there was an Alfa-Romeo parked in front of the gate. "Do you know," exclaimed Miriam, "I think that's Xavier's car!"

They went in through the gate, and walking up through the orchard toward the house Brendan realized its strangeness was caused by the heavy green wooden shutters having been swung shut on all the windows. And there was Xavier sitting Indian fashion on the terrace amid his baggage and with his dog barking at them.

"What are you doing here?" Brendan called out.

"Mother's liver is uncurable," he answered, standing up. He and Mimi embraced, and he kissed Brendan on both cheeks, family style.

"I thought maybe you had split," he went on, "the house is shut up so tight."

"Where's Neville?" asked Mimi.

Brendan shrugged. "Search me."

"All right," said Xavier eagerly, starting to go through his pockets. You had to be careful what you said around Xavier.

"Did you just abandon your mother in Vichy?" inquired Miriam, pleased at the idea.

"Yeah. I'm just not sick enough to stay in that burg. So I beat it." Xavier had been partly educated in the States, so his English was fluent and his slang dated.

"I didn't bring my keys. Let's see if the doors are all locked."

They were. Brendan knew Neville would not leave an unsealed door or window. And he knew the Mas Tranquilitat well enough to know that it could not be forced in any way with anything less than a field gun. Where the hell was Neville? The one time when his presence was necessary, he vanished.

So they all sat down on the terrace. Xavier's dog, Titus, licked Brendan's face experimentally. He patted this big strong figure of a German shepherd.

After a while dusk settled in, and Brendan began to get seriously concerned. Had something happened to Neville? Or had he absconded with their passports and traveler's checks and the Mas silver? He had come with the house, and highly recommended. But anything was possible in the South of France.

Eventually an old taxi rattled into view and stopped at the lower gate. Someone got out, surveyed the parked cars and them sitting on the terrace; it must be Neville—carrying something rather large, Brendan thought. The taxi was paid, and as the old car backed and turned to drive away, the figure moved across the road into the woods, then almost immediately reappeared, came through the gate, and up through the orange trees toward them.

It was Neville.

"I'm sorry, monsieur," he said through scarcely moving lips, eyes on the ground. "Took my day off, since you and Miss Lucas were going to the hills."

"Yes. Just tell me in advance, though, will you, so I can keep from getting locked out. And I don't think you have to shut the house up like a fortress when it's going to be empty for only a few hours. Looks as though you expected the Algerians to storm it."

His face suggested that this was a distinct possibility.

Brendan introduced him to Xavier, whom he immediately began calling Monsieur the Duke.

"Not Monsieur le Duc, Neville. My father is the Marquis de Dornay, and I have the title of Comte de Dornay, but all of those titles were abolished a long time ago."

"Yes, Monsieur the Count," answered Neville stiffly. Titles had not been abolished as far as *he* was concerned. Why, such an offhand attitude as Xavier's might be extended to take in questioning the legitimacy of the Queen!

They went into the house, entering then for the first time its shuttered somberness, dim, reverberating, its Mediterranean-gray woodwork strangely institutional-looking, as though the house had become some kind of clinic, a retreat perhaps for nerve cases. It was empty and echoing and twilighted. Changed and shuttered, it seemed to brood over an inner silence.

Brendan asked Neville to put Xavier's bags in Mimi's room.

Neville looked as though he had been spat at. Then, very cautiously, as though he expected the order to be countermanded at any moment, he carried it out.

Xavier, deeply amused, watched. "He's shocked as hell," he remarked gleefully. "How anybody in the South of France could be shocked by a man sleeping with a woman escapes me. Now, if you'd said, 'Put Monsieur Farel's bags in *my* room,' I can see he might hesitate for an instant. But just an instant."

"What if you'd said," put in Mimi, " 'Neville, take Monsieur Farel's bags to your own room and turn down the bed?' "

"Maybe that's what he was waiting for," said Xavier with mock thoughtfulness. That was typical Xavier irreverence, Brendan reflected.

Irreverence, Brendan recalled as they moved into the living room, was a way of life with Xavier Farel de Dornay. Literally nothing was sacred: his mother's liver, the Catholic Church, General de Gaulle, baseball, jet travel, Van Gogh, French perfume, camembert, Joan of Arc, German shepherds, France, his title, his mother's title, Brigitte Bardot, the Louvre, democracy, Algerians, his car, Russia, doctors, the Kennedy family, cats, himself, Miriam, her mother, Brendan—all were tenpins set up expressly to be knocked down by his irreverence.

"You're not looking your best," Xavier said, fixing his shiny dark eyes on Brendan.

Xavier was tall and slim, and tended to dress either very elegantly or else like a bum. Today he was pre-

sentable in tan sports shirt and slacks. He did not
show it particularly but he was very strong physically, and went in for car racing and steeplechases
and hunting. That was the side of him which
charmed everybody, that and his clean-cut good
looks.

Neville served them a very good dinner—sole
amandine—and after bringing coffee went back
into the kitchen. A minute later he came back into
the dining room. Leaning down close to Brendan's
ear he murmured, "There seems to be something
on the hill behind us I think you should see, monsieur."

"On the hill? What kind of a something?"

His unwavering face remained close. "I think you
should come and have a look, monsieur."

Brendan got up, shrugged at the others, and followed him into the kitchen. Neville indicated the
open kitchen door and Brendan stepped through it
and looked up at the hill.

Rising above the dark bulk of the hill there was a
great tower of smoke, much darker than the hill or
the night sky. Glinting through the trees on the horizon here and there were edges and tongues of fire,
the incinerating wildness loose in the hills.

Xavier was standing behind them. "We'd better
go," he murmured. "They'll need volunteers."

"Yes."

"What about me?" asked Mimi piteously, who was
standing behind Xavier.

"You," said Xavier, smiling and taking hold of her
chin. "Women don't fight forest fires, not in France
anyway."

"But I don't want—"

They were already hurrying upstairs to put on some boots. Mimi followed.

"But I'll be left—"

"Hmmm? Should we take an ax, Denny?"

"I don't know if there is one."

"But I could stay in the car—"

"That's not sensible, Mimi. We may need all the space in the car to take men from one place to another." They went down to the front terrace, Titus madly at their heels every step of the way. They looked up at the smoke and what fire was visible. It was quite a distance away and the wind seemed to be pushing it eastward, in the direction of Nice. Anyone who had lived here as much as Brendan had to know a lot about forest fires. They were an annual menace. The dried-out summer trees, the capricious Mediterranean winds, one untended camper's fire, and thousands and thousands of acres could be burned out, homes destroyed, people trapped and burned to death.

"I think this house is in no danger at all," he said to Mimi. "And if the wind did shift, Neville could lead you in a minute and a half through that big drainage pipe below the grove and you'd be in that stone village with the big stone wall around it that no forest fire could get into."

"I know I'm safe from the *forest fire* . . ."

"Well then."

"I don't like to be left alone," she murmured pleadingly.

"What do you mean, alone? There's Neville, and there's Titus here."

"Yes, miss," said Neville from the door, "I'll keep a lookout."

Mimi embraced Xavier tightly. She kissed Brendan. Then she set her shoulders, turned, and leading Titus by the collar, went back into the Mas Tranquilitat.

They drove off in search of the front where organized fighting would be going on.

"I thought of telephoning the firehouse or the police to find out where," Brendan said as Xavier forced the Alfa in a controlled careening along the narrow, steep and curving roads, "but the line was sure to be busy, and besides, these fires can move so fast. Nobody knows where they're fighting it except the people who are there."

After they had driven about ten minutes the woods on both sides of the road suddenly disappeared and two black fields, charred, dead and smoldering, replaced them. An onslaught of flames had passed this way and gone. Then the trees reappeared on both sides. There was a tight curve ahead, and there the terrain was totally burned out in all directions. The leavings of some small structure slumped near the curve in the road.

They roared on and suddenly there were parked cars and then abruptly hoses and fire engines and a horde of hustling men. They left the car by the side of the road and joined them.

The next hours moved confusedly by in a scramble of lugging heavy hoses from place to place, driving at top speed from one breakthrough by the fire to another, hanging around the streets of the little town of Biot while someone decided where they should go next. Then on one excursion they were suddenly confronted by the conflagration itself, in a clearing just off the road; there it was, the leaping famished enemy, loose, darting and chewing and broiling its way at them, the heat of it scorching their faces, and behind it a house they had come to try to save, wrecked, the owners standing out of the way in the road, not looking. Firemen brought up hoses and they pulled and lugged them into position and the fire hesitated, receded a little, eventually subsided and died out. The wind had lessened, the house was gone, the forest decimated.

The strange smells of charred wood and floating ashes and burned earth were the normal smells of life to them by the time dawn began to creep over the black deadness. The fire had moved out of the area; it was not extinguished, flaring on toward Nice, but with the ordeal over in this area they turned back to the Mas Tranquilitat through the pure splendor of another Mediterranean dawn.

The Mas glowed and sparkled in the long Italianate morning rays, celebrating, showing its morning face, effulgent, indestructible. No forest fire was going to efface its stony presence.

Xavier and Brendan found Mimi in the living room, huddled in a green robe on a sofa sipping coffee, Titus curled on the floor in front of her. "Hello," she said in her low-pitched voice, gazing at them over the rim of her coffee cup.

"Hello yourself," replied Xavier cheerily.

"Nobody *says* that any more, Xavier," Brendan said irritably.

"I don't mind," said Miriam. "But something I do mind . . ."

"Yes?" said Xavier, sitting next to her, putting his arm around her, kissing her.

Brendan was so tired that he was registering impressions with exceptional clarity. Exhaustion had removed inhibitions and qualifications and enabled him to see very penetratingly.

He saw as Xavier put his arm around her and pecked her cheek that he had never believed in the sincerity of Xavier's public displays of affection toward Miriam. They had always looked stagy to him.

Did he really not care for her, or was it the streak of reticence, privacy in his nature? When they were alone, then did he truly give and take love?

"Never mind what I do mind," said Mimi a little archly.

If she's going to be coy I'm going to strangle her, Brendan thought; he was close to complete exhaustion.

"Was it exciting?" she asked Xavier.

"Oh, in a way," he said judiciously. "People's homes being burned to the ground, that held my interest for a little bit, broiled horses—"

She punched him. "You know what I mean. The experience, the teamwork . . ."

"Um-hum," Brendan said, slumping onto a stool. "Where's Neville?"

"I don't know," said Mimi.

"What do you mean? Has he gone out?"

"I don't know. After you left he—well, he began shutting the house up, the way it was earlier today, when Xavier got here. All the shutters closed and everything. I began to feel claustrophobic. So I said, 'Neville, you don't have to do that. That won't keep the forest fire out if it comes our way.' 'Yes, miss,' he said, and went on shutting the place up. I went into the library to see if I could get any news of the fire on television. No luck, just those abominable French TV shows—someday they'll spend more than fifteen cents on a French TV show and then they'll have a smash hit. And when I came back in here I found the house shut up like a tomb. Echoing. Titus looked suspicious, ears back, snooping around. I called for Neville. Nothing. I looked in the kitchen, knocked on his bedroom door, looked upstairs. No Neville. Then I began to get a little terrified." She put down her cup and began slowly massaging her cheeks, as though to bring color back into them. "I didn't know what I was more afraid of—being alone in this empty mausoleum with fire loose around it, or having *Neville* drifting around locking things up. So I proceeded to open up the shutters again. I went up to my room and changed into this, tried to read for a while. Around midnight or maybe later I came down to get a glass of vichy water and goddamnit if the house wasn't all closed up again! Every shutter. All lights out. All the inside doors have locks on them—did you notice that?—and every last one of them was locked. By this time I was so nervous I didn't open things again. Didn't even go as far as the kitchen. I just took Titus, darling Titus here"—she caressed his head fondly and he looked worshipfully up at her—"and went back to my room and got into bed and under the covers. What's going on around here?"

"He's just conscientious, overconscientious," Brendan said.

"Well, Mr. Conscientious deserted the house in the

middle of a forest fire." She got up. "I'll fix you some coffee." Then going out the door she remarked over her shoulder, "I think he thinks this is his house."

A minute or two later Xavier said, "Maybe he does."

They trailed out into the kitchen and began fumbling in the cupboards and refrigerator while Miriam made the coffee. No one spoke.

A key scraped in the great wooden door outside the inner, glass-topped kitchen door. It swung open. Neville was standing there in the kitchen garden. He slowly unlocked the inner door and came in. There was a moment of indecisive silence.

"Well, Neville," Brendan said, "we were wondering where you were."

Neville looked very briefly at all three of them. The set expression on his face was unreadable. In his exhausted state Brendan suddenly thought: He's hidden his feelings from people all his life. "I went up to the top of the hill," Neville said in his distant voice, "to keep a lookout. In case the fire started to come this way. Closed up the house good and tight first."

Brendan gave Mimi a look: You see, the conscientious servant. She looked unblinkingly back at him.

"Can I prepare you something?" he went on quietly.

"Yes! Breakfast! Up on my balcony." Brendan was getting his second or third or fourth wind. "Come on," he called to the others. "You too, Titus."

So they went upstairs, Xavier and Brendan took showers, and then they all had a gala breakfast on the balcony—"Bring us some of that champagne, Neville!"—as morning spread and splashed its purest colors across the white and green of Cannes below, and moved on toward Spain.

Behind them, out of sight, the black slow column of smoke still hung its pall over the South of France.

CHAPTER
THREE

BRENDAN LUCAS felt that he was finishing growing up at last. Perhaps it was his being the undisputed master of this large house that created, or at least reinforced that feeling. He was the boss.

The narrow, four-storied Georgetown house where he had started growing up was elegant but cramped, his bedroom small, his hi-fi necessarily tuned low, the subdued tone of the household set to soothe his temperamental father. Brendan felt he had had no chance to be, or even to search for, himself; that had been his real preoccupation in the years since. He believed that he had been making progress, but knew he still had a very considerable distance to go.

Xavier Farel de Dornay had been an important

stage in that search. "Xavier the Savior," as they had called him at Georgetown University, merited that nickname through a kind of given certitude he seemed to possess about himself. The Savior *knew* that sports were a ridiculous waste of time, an adolescent American aberration he, the Comte de Dornay, wouldn't waste a second engaging in, much less watching or discussing.

At one time, during their sophomore year at Georgetown, the Savior had been a Marxist, and had exerted sufficient influence on Brendan to move him leftward from Eisenhower Republicanism to Stevensonian Democracy, but no further.

Although Xavier detested organized sports he loved to exercise, and this often took the form of wrestling with Brendan. Taller and heavier, the Savior usually won. Brendan didn't mind too much losing to him, since they were such good friends. Once Mimi, a budding, shapely seventeen, walked into their dormitory room while they, in shorts, were struggling on the floor. "You look ridiculous," she snapped. "What are you doing? Why don't you grow up!"

Brendan almost never invited Xavier to visit the Georgetown house because the Georgetown house and its occupants, except for Mimi, were what he was consciously trying to grow away from, surmount, and Xavier was one of the influences he had enlisted in that effort. Therefore his mother had never become really acquainted with Xavier.

Xavier the Savior was a French cynic, from birth apparently, with something ardent and genuine buried at his core.

"Let's go and get laid," he said to Brendan at lunch the day after the forest fire.

Mimi dropped her spoon and glared. "That's not funny," she said harshly.

"Well, maybe you want to go and get laid too," Xavier added, rolling his eyes at her.

"You've just grossed me out with that remark," said Brendan.

"Don't like the thought, do you?" said Xavier, now rolling his eyes at Brendan.

Neville brought in the main course. "What have we for dessert?" Brendan asked him loudly.

"Savory, monsieur."

Miriam felt the stillness of the Mediterranean summer afternoon was surrounding the coast and the Mas and her bedroom and herself. She had been lying on the terrace with Xavier earlier and now she felt suffused inside by this shadowless southern sun. Xavier's impossible remarks at lunch . . . never mind, anything to be irreverent, provocative . . . the coolness of the bedspread and of the heavily shuttered room . . . she felt like the princess in the tower, the sleeping beauty, Margot Fonteyn awaiting Rudolf Nureyev . . . so deliciously sleepy . . . two glasses of wine at lunch and her featherhead was ready to pass into a long summer's nap . . . a dancer spinning somewhere . . . the sun spinning . . . turning, turning . . . staccato feet pounding on wood . . . uh . . . it was the door of her bedroom, a discreet tapping. Lurching back into consciousness, very annoyed, she said, "Yes? Who is it?"

"It's Neville, miss."

"Neville! What do you want!"

"Monsieur the Count's buuh—"

"What? I can't hear you. Open the door."

Neville took one short step into the room. "I am sorry, miss, so sorry. Did I disturb you? Monsieur the Count asked me to polish his riding boots and this is the only hour today I have for that. They *are* in here . . . if you don't mind . . ."

"Yes," she said shortly. "They're in here. In that closet, I think."

"I'm so sorry, miss, if I woke you from your nap. And you ladies of the theater do need your rest, I know."

He crossed to the closet, got the boots and tiptoed out.

Mimi turned abruptly from her back onto her side, but the sun suffusion, the towered princess, the spinning and the sleep would not come back to the lady of the theater.

"I'm so very sorry I disturbed you this afternoon, miss."

"Never mind, Neville." She had cut some flowers from the Mas's small garden and was arranging them on the dining room table before dinner.

"That room is so small, cramped," he went on.

"What room?"

"That—your—where you were taking your nap, miss."

"I haven't noticed."

"If you wanted to move," he began very tentatively, "to one of the empty back bedrooms . . ."

She sucked in a breath. What was this zany trying

to do now? She had not been in the rough give-and-take of the theater for nothing, and crisply she said, "If Xavier and I need any rearranging done, Neville, we'll let you know."

"Oh, of course, miss."

And no rearranging of the bedroom was done. But at dinner, glancing at the flowers, Mimi had a definite feeling that *they* had been rearranged. Or was it just that they looked so different by candlelight?

"Tell me about your life together as children," Xavier said, leaning forward eagerly, his hands clasped low between his knees. They were sitting in the softly lit living room late in the evening.

"Well, we were thrown together more than most brothers and sisters," said Brendan, "because in the middle of growing up we were uprooted from Georgetown—"

"And suddenly we were living here," Mimi continued, "well, in Nice, surrounded by people speaking *French!*"

"So we had no friends, just the family and some other American families. We were thrown together a lot."

"It was hell," said Mimi slyly.

"It wasn't really," said Brendan sincerely.

Mimi sighed.

Neville was moving softly back and forth along the back hallway, putting away some linen he had laundered.

"But getting back to your childhood together," went on Xavier. "Were you very close?"

"Mmm," said Mimi noncommittally.

"I guess so," said Brendan.

"Did you ever massage her legs?"

"What?"

"Did you ever give her a massage? She always needs massages."

"No, of course not!"

"Why 'of course not'? Why so indignant?"

"Well I don't—well . . ."

"Mother did it," Mimi cut in. "When I needed it, which wasn't often in those days. Youthful muscles."

"Y–e–e–s–s," said Xavier, rubbing his large hands together. "All those youthful, sisterly muscles!"

"Spear fishing!" announced Brendan the next morning. "Today we're going spear fishing!"

"Of course," said Xavier.

"My class . . ." said Mimi uncertainly.

"Forget it," Xavier said.

"Neville!" Brendan called out, exhilarated as always by the anticipation of any sea excursion.

"Monsieur?" Neville was very promptly at his side.

"Make us up a lunch, something we can eat on a boat at sea."

"Yes, monsieur. Perhaps some chicken salad, sliced tomatoes—"

"*Very* Anglo-Saxon," countered Xavier. "Why not some salami and cheese and bread—*French* bread—and some good Algerian red, eh?"

"Okay, something." Brendan's mind was far from food; already he saw the smokily blue depths of the Mediterranean, the silvery schools of little fish turning suddenly in unison as on some magic command, the subaqueous sunlight glittering along their sides.

Going upstairs to change into bathing suits Mimi murmured to Brendan, "Why don't we take Neville along?"

"Huh? Neville? I thought you didn't like being around him—Petrouchka . . ."

"I don't like being around him *alone*. But I don't mind with you and Xavier. He does look so pale. You're always trying to get him to go out, stop puttering around this house."

"You're right."

By the time they got ready to go and came back downstairs Neville had been into the village and bought what was needed for lunch. To Brendan's surprise he quietly demurred at the invitation to join them. "So much to do here," he murmured. But Brendan sensed a not-quite-interred desire to make the excursion, and when Mimi and Xavier joined in urging him Neville slowly agreed. It took even longer to persuade him to change into a swimsuit but eventually he agreed to that too.

"This will give him a little refreshment," said Miriam, when he had gone to his room to change. "Anybody would go completely bonkers cooped up here slaving away all day—and half the night. You'll see. The food will be even better."

Neville came out wearing vintage swimming trunks, black and rather long, with a white belt. On his feet he wore rubber beach slippers. He also had on a Hawaiian aloha shirt blazing with an orange and pink flowered pattern.

"That shirt!" exclaimed Xavier. "It's a knockout!"

"Oh, Monsieur the Count, you know I travel so much. Try to buy a souvenir everywhere. Is it too vulgar? I'll go change."

"No, no, it's right on the button, isn't it, Mimi?"

"Right on the button," she repeated dryly. "Nothing's right on the button any more, Monsieur the Count. It's cool."

"Actually, miss," volunteered Neville, "it's a little heavy."

"I like it," said Brendan. "Let's go."

They drove down to the Port of Antibes and set out to sea in a thirty-five-foot motor cruiser owned and piloted by a longstanding Provençal friend of Brendan's known as Loulou. The name of this new motor cruiser was the *Ringaling.*

"Where did you get that name?" Brendan asked Loulou.

"It's the name of a circus," he replied proudly, "a famous *American* circus! You mean you never heard of it!"

"Ringaling? Oh yes, of course, Ringaling Brothers and Barkum and Gaily."

"That's it. The best, no?"

"Oh sure. The best. Absolutely."

"The Big Top, eh?"

"How did you ever think to name it that?"

"I rent the boat to underseas divers, and many of them are Americans visiting here, and they say that they always have a circus with me and that I must call it Ringaling and so I do."

"Great. We'll have a circus today, too."

"Who's that guy?" inquired Loulou in his crackling, humorous voice, cocking his head in the direction of Neville.

"He works at my house. Cook."

"Cook! But he can't even speak French!"

"All the same he's the cook."

Loulou's tanned, crinkled face studied Brendan's. "It's unheard-of. Where does he buy his clothes—in the Flea Market?"

"It wouldn't surprise me."

"Why don't you come to me if you're looking for a cook? I could find you someone first-class, making the real Provençal dishes."

"Well, you see . . . Neville came with the house."

Neville was sitting on the gunwale rather near them, his head up, nose in the wind, fixed expression. Surely, Brendan thought, he couldn't hear their voices over the boat's engine, or even if he could, he wouldn't understand this rapid exchange.

And then he thought: The hell with Neville; we're at sea.

Brendan had suddenly realized one day not long before that all of his ancestors came from the British Isles, either Ireland or England, so that not one of them could have lived at any time in his or her life far from the sea. The sea girt every living one of them all their lives and its verge was both the limit of their Irish and English destinies and the avenue to all future external possibilities, an avenue which those of them who were to be his immediate ancestors eventually took to America.

There was one exception among this tree of Anglo-Irish forebears: according to fairly well-founded family tradition, reinforced by some definitely Iberian traces in his sister's appearance, one of their ancestors was Spanish. Yet he only reinforced the sea urge in the blood, having reached Ireland as a shipwrecked member of the Spanish Armada.

Perhaps it is he who put into Brendan's psyche the

qualifying condition of his sea urge: above all others, it was the Mediterranean Sea which meant most to him, the sea itself, the look of it, and the kind of food people around it ate, and their music and dancing, and what they drank, and a kind of very non-Irish, un-English starkness in their character.

The *Ringaling* breasted over some long rollers as they moved out from the port, the sea slid silkily beneath them, stirring in Brendan memories of a thousand fresh mornings in his young life in the South of France, in the Flower Market in Nice with Mimi, driving toward the Alps for a day's skiing, buying a peach at an outdoor stall, reading *Nice-Matin* or the *International Herald-Tribune* on the terrace of a café as the assiduous French waiters scrubbed the pavement almost into powder, the freshness of Creation everywhere: the Mediterranean world, blue and light gold, ineffable, where life was best lived.

"Monsieur," murmured Neville, close to his ear to be heard above the engine, "I bought some oil for your skin. The sun is so hot at sea. Reflects off the water. Can be dangerous. I know from my time in the merchant navy."

"Good idea." Standing in his swim trunks Brendan rubbed the oil on his face, arms and chest.

"Permit me," murmured Neville, and as Brendan stood shifting from foot to foot Neville spread some oil over his shoulders and back.

"Give me some of that!" called out Xavier.

Neville gave him the bottle and he covered the front of himself with oil. Then, turning, he handed it to Brendan for his back. Neville withdrew.

"Mmm, feels good," said Xavier. "Now I'm going to slither in the water, like an eel!"

"Give me some, too!" called out Mimi, and Brendan and Xavier playfully charged at her and took turns splashing the oil over her body. "Not in my eyes, dummy," she said to Brendan.

When she was well coated, Neville retrieved the bottle of oil from where Xavier had dropped it and withdrew to the tiny galley belowdecks.

About half an hour out from shore they arrived at an underwater reef. Here Loulou anchored. The *Ringaling* carried complete diving equipment. "What's that!" said Mimi as she saw Xavier and Brendan struggling into harnesses with heavy air tanks attached.

"Well, we're going down to almost a hundred feet, of course," explained Xavier. "Want to come?"

"A hundred feet! Me! Are you crazy? Of course I don't want to come."

"Here you are, mademoiselle," said Loulou in French. "Mask, kick.fins, breathing tube. You can float on the surface and see many beautiful things through your mask."

An annoyed, bewildered look came into her face. "You mean you two are going away adventuring and leave me alone *again!* No, it's too much."

Brendan looked kindly at her, but what was to be done? She had no training in undersea diving, and neither brotherly love nor sibling loyalty nor anything else was going to come between him and the depths of the sea on this morning in the South of France. "Loulou, will you accompany Mimi? Or perhaps Neville . . ."

Neville had materialized on deck again. "Can't

swim, monsieur," he murmured apologetically.

"It's all right, Neville," Mimi said shortly. "Well then, Monsieur Loulou, it's you and me. These two here," she cocked an eloquent hand, palm upward, at Xavier and Brendan, "these two inseparable schoolboys, they're off again. *Au revoir, bébés.*"

Brendan, looking at no one and saying nothing, worked assiduously at putting on the undersea gear.

He and Xavier then seated themselves on the side of the boat, backs to the sea. Brendan signaled Xavier with a nudge and then they both fell overboard backwards, so that the tanks on their backs took the slap of hitting the sea. Immediately they were in the sun-suffused flux just below the surface. The hiss of breathing in the air from the tank, the shuddering gurgle of exhalation, these were now the sole sounds in their world. The sounds were those of patients on operating tables. Brendan and Xavier worked themselves deeper by slow stages, from time to time equalizing the pressure inside their heads by "clearing" their ears.

They floated slowly past the craggy, ghost-white sides of the coral reef, through schools of tiny transparent fish, silver towers of bubbles rising and spreading from the backs of their heads toward the surface, the light around them growing mistier, the thickness of the heavy layer of water above them slowing their minds and movements, estranging them from those beings who lived in air—corrupt, these earth-people seemed now, over-fecund, prone to dirty skin . . . shrill voices. All these earthbound traits faded as the two friends explored along the vaults of the sea.

Brendan now began to play at the quality he enjoyed most in diving: weightlessness. He pulled himself down along the flank of the reef headfirst and then stopped and just hung there for a while staring at a waving coral frond. Then he slowly somersaulted, seeing the vast blue expanse of water extending to the glowing surface. He drifted along sideways, the water slowing his movements so that all of them were forced to be graceful: he was in fact dancing.

Xavier's long body drifted just above him; they drifted along together, dulled and content, sealed off, free.

Then after a while they slowly began to rise back to reality; once again the air inside their heads had to be slowly readjusted, this time to the lightening pressure of the water around them which also grew warmer as they neared the surface, becoming more mundane, less mysterious, bits of seaweed and other flotsam loose in it.

They broke through into the blinding sunlight and tossing surface of the Mediterranean, and the dive was over.

Neville's lunch turned out to be cold ham, potato salad, French bread and white wine. It was about half what he had planned, half what Xavier had wanted. Brendan reflected that in some ways Neville had the qualities of a successful diplomat.

That night when they were alone on the terrace of the Mas Tranquilitat, Brendan said to Xavier, "You're jealous of my closeness to Mimi, aren't you?"

"Yes."

"You know that you don't have any reason to be."

"In some part of my mind I'm suspicious about everybody."

"You know you don't have any reason to be, about me."

In their room that night Mimi said to Xavier, "Sometimes you seem almost *too* close, you and Brendan."

"Hm?"

"Neville gave you both a very funny look when you insisted that Denny put the sun oil on your back."

"I didn't insist. It was just natural."

"Natural. Well, he gave you a very funny look."

"Neville is sick."

"Yes, but is he the only one?"

"It isn't Neville who's suspecting something, is it?" said Xavier slowly. "Or if it is, who cares. It's you."

Brendan went to his vast bedroom alone that night as on all nights. He could hear the blurred voices of Mimi and Xavier from their room. In the bottom of his Catholic mind he felt a tinge of guilt, a touch of shame, for allowing his sister and a man to sleep together under his roof when they weren't married. He thought this attitude of his to be old-fashioned and stupid, but he was the result of his ancestors and who they were and what they believed.

That was the only reason he resented Mimi and Xavier sleeping together night after night in the next room, wasn't it? Lying in bed alone, Brendan asked himself that.

CHAPTER
FOUR

FOUR DAYS later Mrs. Marietta Lucas arrived at nine o'clock in the morning unannounced. "I didn't know I could get out of Washington, and then I just found I could at the last moment yesterday, so I got right on a plane last night. Where is my room? Show me the bedrooms." They were standing on the terrace and she was already on the outside stone stairway leading up to Mimi and Xavier's room.

"No!" Brendan cried. Then more calmly, "Not that way. That's uh, condemned, that stairway."

"This? Solid as a rock. It is a rock. How could it be condemned? Are you making fun of me, young man?"

"Mother, listen," he improvised. "Not now. Neville

—he's the houseman and cook and as they say a jewel —wouldn't like us butting in just now. Come on in and sit down and he'll take your bags and arrange everything."

It worked. Five years in the Diplomatic Service had not gone for nothing.

A few minutes later Mimi excused herself. She went upstairs and swiftly sorted out the sleeping arrangements. Neville wordlessly, coolly, even she sensed contemptuously, assisted her. She felt her Spanish temper starting to rise against his tacit disapproval of her and Xavier sleeping together—who did he think he *was* around here!—but there wasn't time to do anything about that. When they had finished one would never have known that Mimi and Xavier had held hands.

After Mrs. Lucas "freshened up," as she put it, and had a bite of breakfast, Brendan took her for a stroll through the orchard.

She had never told him nor anyone else her age but his calculations indicated she must be around fifty-five. Mr. Lucas had been killed in the crash of a private airplane six years before. He left her with an income of around seventeen thousand dollars a year. She resumed the work she had done before marriage, and off and on during it: professional research. She worked for authors and historians and politicians, and the only complaint Brendan had ever heard about her work was that she was *too* thorough, she dug up literally everything. Winnowing out was not her forte; she did exactly, but exactly what was asked of her, fulfilled to and beyond the letter.

She had always been interested in women's rights.

She was active in the League of Women Voters, in the Republican party, specializing in women's affairs, and was now moving toward favoring a kind of asexual Women's Liberation. There had always been a businesswoman lurking inside her even in her most matronly married days, a brisk, take-charge quality. She was someone who could add up a column of figures like lightning; she even had a certain grasp of what went on under the hood of her car.

"She's not really going to marry this Xavier, is she?" were her opening words for the stroll.

"She is, I think. Why shouldn't she?"

"Well . . . if she wants to be his body servant all her life . . ."

"He's very intelligent," Brendan said, "and witty, and, well, I think she loves him very much, and that's the most important thing, isn't it?"

She pulled one of the sour little oranges off a tree and frowned at it. "And does he love her?"

"Of course," he answered quickly.

"The French are a different sort of people. It's hard to be sure what they're feeling. I know. I lived here."

No word for lonely; no word for home.

"So have I."

"You were just a child."

"An adolescent. The most impressionable years."

"Well then, tell me, what's *your* impression of Xavier?"

He hesitated.

His mother was rather tall, with short gray-black hair. She was a strider, wore sensible shoes, good conservative clothes, and reminded many people a little of Eleanor Roosevelt. She played a give-no-quarter brand of tough-minded golf and had beaten him at it many times. Xavier had visited her and Mimi in her house in Georgetown several months earlier, and there her impression of him had clearly formed and set. And when her impression was set, it was set.

Knowing this so well, Brendan thought it a waste of energy to try to dissuade her. "I like him a lot," he contented himself with saying. "He's got his problems. Who hasn't? He—"

"Such as?" She stopped walking.

"Oh, well . . ." Why had he said that? Because basically he *was* concerned, very much, about Mimi marrying Xavier, and wanted some close consultation and advice from someone qualified. The trouble was, his mother wasn't qualified. Hers was an open-and-shut, black-and-white, good-and-bad view of human beings. "Oh, well . . . he's—well, he's kind of high-strung and I guess you'd say nervous—"

"Unstable."

"I didn't say that."

"These self-indulgent so-called 'good' families. I've seen a lot of them. They come and go in Washington, in the embassies. If they're French their liver is *always* weak. Inherited from ten generations of over-eaters and overdrinkers. How is his liver? Well, I know it is bad. Never mind. But his nerves." She was silent for a moment. "That's just—well, people have to get a grip on themselves. Not let their feelings run away with them. Then their nerves will take care of themselves."

He looked at her. She really believed that.

Then she asked quietly, "Has he ever been institutionalized?"

As a matter of fact he had been, once, in the

French army, "for observation," yet was very soon
released and he served out his military term. But
Brendan was not going to tell Madame Implacable
here that.

"Has he undergone treatment?"

"I don't think so. I said he was nervous sometimes.
I didn't say he was crazy, for God's sake. Listen,
Mother, you're honestly making much too much out
of this. He's a little high-strung, that's all. Finely
bred, like a race horse."

"Mmmm." She was thinking.

"I'd like to see the house," she said late in the
afternoon after taking a nap.

With his mother that did not mean seeing the
rooms they lived in and used; that meant every nook
and cranny, attic to cellar. They started in the attic,
which Brendan had never seen. The door leading to
it was locked. Neville came with the key, and opened
the door to the stairs leading upward. "There's nothing you'll want to see up there," he said and started
to close the door, but she was already on the move.
They all mounted to the attic. The one naked light
bulb was turned on. Although there were dormers at
this level on the exterior of the house, the attic was
windowless because opaque tiles had been fitted into
the openings. Brendan wondered why.

"Security, I suppose," Neville answered his question. "Greater security."

The owner of the house, one Frédéric Boileau,
Parisian lawyer, seemed to have had an absolute
mania for security.

There were a few old pieces of furniture, some

tattered books, a certain amount of dust. Mrs. Lucas nosed here and there, making small indeterminate noises, and then they descended to the second floor. Neville went on down to the kitchen. She opened the door and walked into Mimi's room. Mimi was at her dressing table, and looked startled as she caught sight of them in her mirror. Xavier was standing nearby.

"Well," said her mother, "don't you have a nice big room here." She had flushed slightly on entering.

"Yes, isn't it!" said Mimi brightly.

Mrs. Lucas looked at the bedspreads and the pictures, admired the view down over Cannes, examined the outside stairway which "can't possibly have been condemned. It's like Gibraltar!"

"That was just a joke," mumbled Brendan.

She went through the connecting bathroom ("Plenty of hot water?" "Plenty.") and into his bedroom, and on through the rest of that floor, inspecting each of the back three bedrooms and the second bathroom.

Then they descended to the first floor, and once she had admired the library and revisited the living room and dining room they went through the pantry and up to the shut kitchen door. She opened that and walked in. Neville was frowning over some sauce on the stove and took several seconds to turn and look at them. "And this is where all the good things come from!" cried Mrs. Lucas.

"Yes," Neville said very quietly through an unmoving mouth.

"My, look at the old-fashioned stove. And I hear you can make such good things on it."

"Yes."

"What's that you're cooking now?"

"Preparing a sauce for the rabbit."

"Rabbit!"

"Yes, madam, for dinner."

"I can't eat that," she said in a very audible aside to Brendan.

"It's a specialty here in France. You remember."

"I remember we had beef and ham and chickens and chops and other good things your father got for me through our embassy and the Navy."

"Well, Neville, you'll have something else for Mother. The rest of us like rabbit."

"Yes."

"Look at all these pots and pans, will you?" There was a long row of copper pans in all shapes and sizes, and a big square copper brazier. There were several huge aluminum pots, and strainers, spatulas, a chopping block, shredders and scrapers, huge butcher knife, meat cleaver. A meat sauce was very slowly simmering on the back of the stove; this kitchen was never still.

"It smells so good in here," she said. Peering into the refrigerator, she fished around in it and noted some homemade liver pâté.

Neville, poker-stiff, his back turned to her rummaging, went on stirring his sauce.

"Let me show you the rest of the house," Brendan said to her.

"This is the most important room," she observed.

"Yes, it certainly is," he agreed.

Her remark, intended to compliment and mollify Neville, made no visible impression. Were we beginning to court our servant American style, Brendan wondered, instead of ordering him around *à la fran-*

çaise? He wasn't going to let that happen; it was important to remember, especially with touchy cooks, who was paying whom.

"Interesting," said his mother, going out the other door which led into a back hallway. "Maybe I will just take a nibble of that rabbit tonight."

On the left in the back hall was a broom closet which she inspected, then a lavatory, then a massive back door leading to a small stone back terrace. They made a tour of that and then came back inside. The next and last room on the back corridor, and the only room on this floor they had not visited, was Neville's bedroom. Before he could speak she turned the knob with her habitual confidence. "It's locked," she said, looking puzzled.

"Yes. That's Neville's room. Let's go down and look at the basement."

"Does he have a nice room?"

"I—yes, I think—well, as a matter of fact I haven't been in it. Neville came with the house, so he was here before I was. He seems to be comfortable."

"Aren't you sure?"

"He'd say something if he wasn't."

"Well, in *my* house I would certainly want to see everything and be sure everything was right and as it should be."

Well, this isn't *your house,* he wanted to yell.

"Do you have the key?"

"No. Neville has it, of course."

"Not have a key for a closed, unvisited room in your own house! You see, that comes of having no wife to tend to these things for you. Well, I'll help out, for the time I'm here."

How long, O Lord, how long?

She turned and strode back down the hall to the kitchen. Before he could catch up with her, she stuck her head through the doorway and smiling pleasantly said, "Neville, let me just have the key to your room a minute. I want to be sure you're comfortable. This son of mine . . . so thoughtless."

"That won't be necessary, madam. I'm fine."

"I want to be sure. You're so necessary to this household."

"I'm quite all right. Thank you, madam."

"You men so tend to neglect your own comfort. Get wrapped up in your work." This was in her agreeable tone. Then in her subdued but definite Queen Victoria manner: "The key, please."

Neville's eyes remained on the sauce. To Brendan's amazement he spoke in a completely new voice, one he had never heard before, flatter and louder and earthier. "I won't have anybody going into my room snooping around!"

Her head snapped even further back. "Snooping! I'm looking after my son's house!"

"I don't *want* you to look after it," Brendan exclaimed.

She put one firm hand on his arm to silence him. Her face its severest, her eyes blue ice, she put out her other hand toward Neville and said in her coldest voice, "I am going to require that key."

Neville looked up finally, at Brendan. The eyes, hollow as ever, nevertheless made a kind of appeal and he said, with some expression in his voice for once, a plaintiveness, "Mr. Lucas, I have my rights. Don't I?"

Brendan did not find it easy, even at age twenty-nine, to turn on a mother as willful as his. "Yes, you sure do," he said.

His mother's hand locked like a gauntlet on his arm for an instant and then disdainfully withdrew all physical contact with him, and every other contact. She gave him one look of amazement and accusation.

"We're not going to barge in on your privacy, of course," Brendan added. And then, diplomat to the end, "Someday when you have it the way you want it, give us a glance, why don't you, to see how you're fixed."

Thus being given a suspended sentence, but not a pardon, Neville accepted this for the time being, and resumed his automatic stirring of the sauce.

Marietta Lucas withdrew into the hall, then, opening one of the two big wooden doors, went into the living room.

"I'll be leaving on the late plane today. There's one for New York, I think."

"Oh, please don't start that," Brendan said in exasperation.

"Humiliated by my son in front of a strange servant. I'll *not* put up with it!"

He was now in the mortal bind he had avoided all his life with this impossible woman. Brendan had avoided, feigned, humored, slipped around her. Dealing with her was what landed him in diplomacy. And here it was at long last: her stubborn arrogance against his assertion of himself.

He took a long breath and, with a feeling of riding with an uncontrollable landslide, heard himself say, "We will look into his room. When he's out. We'll

arrange it." He waited for her response, quietly de-
testing himself.

She maintained a long cold silence. Then she said
slowly, "I don't approve of this pampering, not at all.
It leads to bad situations. But, well," in a very dubious
but resigned tone, "if that's the way you want it. It's
your house, heaven knows. I'm just briefly visiting
here. It's your life."

Her tone implied, as it had always implied when
things he did were contrary to her wishes, that his
actions would lead him to the poorhouse or jail or the
insane asylum.

There was a rising tension, a nervousness; hostili-
ties were bubbling toward the surface in the Mas
Tranquilitat as in one of the kettles on Neville's stove.
"Let's go down to the sea again today," Brendan said
at breakfast on the terrace the next morning. He had
slept badly, which was unusual for him, especially
here. It was another shiny, open Mediterranean day.

"What fun," said Mother.

"Take the day off," Brendan said over his shoulder
to Neville as he passed behind him. "We'll have dinner down at the port somewhere."

"Going to be very crowded, monsieur."

"I know some out of the way places . . ."

"Yes."

He was disappointed. It was next to impossible to
pry this man away from his work. Or was it, away
from the Mas? Or what?

They got into the car and took off for the Port of
Antibes, and another day's outing aboard the *Ringaling*.

They cruised off Cap d'Antibes, they snorkled along the reef, they had lunch at sea, all as before. Mrs. Lucas didn't change into a bathing suit but kept out of the sun and spent most of the time reading. Loulou tried to talk to her in French—he tried to talk to everyone—but they had difficulty with each other's accents.

"She's not your mother," he remarked brightly to Brendan afterward.

"Of course she is."

"No," he grinned into the sunshine, "she's not."

The *Ringaling* sliced on through the glittering Mediterranean.

Sometime after lunch Xavier went belowdecks to lie down in the little cabin. There were swells on the sea and he seemed to be feeling a shade queasy. Going to sea had been his idea; it was characteristic of Xavier's convoluted contradictions that he alone was suffering from his own idea. Brendan went down to get himself a glass of water and saw the Savior's long frame in bathing trunks stretched out on a bunk. Mimi, also in a bathing suit, was offering him a towel soaked in cold water to put on his had. "That won't do a bloody bit of good," he growled.

"Well, I don't know what else to do."

"Tell them to take the boat back to the dock and we get off."

"Oh, Xavier, ruin everybody's outing . . ."

"I'm feeling sick."

"I know you are. But if you lie here for a few more minutes . . ."

"How far is it to shore? I'll swim!"

"Don't be silly."

"Oh. Now I'm silly. Well, the hell with it."

He got up unsteadily and headed past Brendan to the little ladder going up on deck. Brendan tried to stop him with his arm. He shoved it out of the way, and Brendan tried to grab him from behind. Xavier wheeled around and nearly took a swing at him. Then he was on deck, saying with his brightest smile to Mrs. Lucas, "Well, goodbye!" and diving clumsily overboard. He surfaced, and began swimming his uncertain crawl toward the tip of Cap d'Antibes, a good mile away.

"Loulou, turn around so we can pick him up."

"Okay."

In a couple of minutes they had maneuvered alongside Xavier. The plunge seemed to have calmed his nerves, the predicament he had plunged into had become clear to him. Brendan knew that he and not Mimi could talk him back into the boat with a minimum loss of face. "Did the swim help?" he asked.

"A little bit."

"Let me give you a hand. We've all had enough sun for one day." Brendan reached out for him. "Where'll we have dinner?" Who knew to what heights his diplomatic career might scale?

"The Hôtel du Cap?" Xavier asked, paddling along.

"Sure. Fine. Uh, how's the water?"

"It's—well, a little colder than I thought, as a matter of fact. Out far from shore like this . . ."

"What *is* going on?" inquired Marietta Lucas, lowering her reading glasses to peer at Xavier.

"Do you want me to help you up now?"

"Okay!"

Back belowdecks Xavier and Miriam continued a very fluent argument in low voices until they reached the dock.

Changing back into street clothes they set out to walk the half-mile or so from the dock to the Hôtel du Cap. Mrs. Lucas found long walks bracing. She went ahead. Brendan forced Xavier to accompany her; he and Mimi followed at a little distance. "When are you two going to get married, anyway? I'm not sure how much longer I can hold this house party together. Too much tension under one roof."

"We can't get married until Xavier's sister gets here."

"When will that be?"

"Oh, any day now. And then we have to get the papers . . ."

"What papers?"

"Lots of papers and certificates and permits. You know France. My being American doesn't help. Xavier has agreed to the Catholic ceremony in addition to the civil one to please Mother. Thank God. Even if he is a left-wing Marxist agnostic Gaullist or something. So that has to be arranged with the priest and—"

"And you've got cold feet."

She walked the peculiar penguin-style walk of the ballet dancer along the road in the afternoon sunshine, streams of cars passing them in both directions, every rocky cranny of the shore below occupied with holiday swimmers.

"It's not that I've got cold feet, it's Xavier . . ."

"You've both got cold feet. Isn't that normal?

Don't most people on the brink of committing themselves to somebody else for life?"

"Not as cold as ours, I expect," she said quietly.
"He's . . . well, you saw yourself today, he *is* difficult,
and *nervous,* and *selfish,* and . . . I don't know . . ."

"I didn't have to see that today. I saw that years
ago. That's Xavier."

She drew a self-encouraging breath, then said quietly, "He does love me."

"Well then."

"Mm. He does love me, and that's almost everything, isn't it?"

"Yes. Almost."

They reached the gracious grounds of the Hôtel du
Cap, beneath the umbrella pines, with the Mediterranean scintillating just below the small cliff at the
bottom of the grounds. At the top of the gently sloping terrain was the delicately rotund old hotel, châ-
teau-like, almost white, fragile, with, for Americans,
the ghosts of the Scott Fitzgeralds and the Gerald
Murphys fading in and out of the brittly elegant,
cavernous old rooms; their wraiths were here, the
wraiths of their innocence and their self-destructive-
ness, hovering over them as they sought in their dif-
fering ways to weave into their fates the elusive
magic of the French South.

Mrs. Lucas and Mimi went into the hotel to take
care of any of those functions the Lucases ag-
glomerated in the phrase "freshen up," and Xavier
and Brendan hastened to the bottom of the grounds
for a stiff drink. "Scotch," Xavier said, "double."

"Me too."

"Your mother doesn't want me to marry her," he
said briefly.

"I—she doesn't? Why not?"

"You know she doesn't. She pretends I'm too decadent or something like that."

"Unstable," Brendan had to murmur.

"Is that what she said?"

"Um-hum."

"Well," he took a long gulp, "that's not her real reason. Her real reason is, she doesn't want to be left alone in the world. Scared stiff of that. Her husband is dead. You have a career which puts you in places like Timbuktu or Katmandu most of the time. That leaves Miriam."

"The Irish," Brendan mused, "always did want to keep one daughter at home as a spinster to take care of the mother."

"That's it."

"But that was when each family had about seven daughters."

"Well, your family has one, so she's elected. And there's Mimi's career. Hard to combine with marriage. Easy with Mother. Mother can *tour* with her. Mother can always be there for Mimi. And Mimi can always be there with Mother. Especially after the career is over. Then Mimi and Mother can settle down in Georgetown forever."

"Beautiful."

"Are you going to let it happen?" Xavier turned his unbeatably handsome face to frown at Brendan.

"Me?"

"You're the man of the family now."

"You don't know Mother."

"I'm beginning to know her. She won't let herself be left alone, I see that in her."

". . . live with you and Mimi . . ."

Xavier cocked a bright, are-you-mad eye at him. Brendan dropped the idea. Nor could she live with him. Their mother's mind was a set of inviolable laws most of which had been forgotten or repealed by the rest of the world, including those nearest her. It was not her tenacious loyalty to these laws which alienated others; it was that she insisted on their enforcement everywhere within her view.

"She was shocked," Brendan went on, "to find you standing, fully clothed and ten feet away to be sure, but still standing in Mimi's bedroom, although Mimi was fully clothed and it was three o'clock in the afternoon."

"If she only knew."

Brendan grabbed his wrist. "She must never know. It's not that it would kill her, as they say. Nothing like that could kill Mother. It's that if she knew, she would have to—she would have to set out to destroy you. And Miriam." He paused. "And me too, because I allowed it to happen under my roof."

Xavier studied his expression.

Mimi and Mrs. Lucas joined them after a while and they wandered eventually up the walk, in the ghostly footsteps of Alexander Woollcott and Grace Moore and the young Hemingway, to have a gracious dinner out of a gracious era, older even than the 1920's, out of the *Belle Epoque,* back now with Marcel Proust and his grandmother at the seaside in the 1880's, back where meal-serving was organized as though it were a military drill by the cadets at St. Cyr, unobtrusive perfection, a lost art remembered here and in a few other châteaux and grand hotels in France, a remembrance of lost time.

Then they drove back, through the passionate

southern night, adrift with pine smells, inextinguish-
able stars, the exhaust fumes of thousands of cars,
uproar, cash, sexuality and nerves, to the Mas Tranquilitat.

Neville was ironing in the kitchen and seemed too
busy to interrupt his work even to greet them. The
barest "Good evening" and he went pounding on
with his iron, perfecting the shape of one of Brendan's shirts.

Once again, very untypically, Brendan had trouble
sleeping that night. Overstimulation? Too much
family? He tossed and wondered until almost dawn.
What was he doing with his life? Why was he really
in the Foreign Service? Why did he repeatedly fall in
love but never get married? Wasn't Xavier the
wrong husband for Mimi? Why had he introduced
them? Wasn't his mother right in her disapproval?
Why had he ever forsaken her standards? What had
he really developed to replace them? What kind of
a Catholic was he? Was he a Catholic at all? Wasn't
sex only successful in marriage? There he was, laps-
ing into his mother's puritanism, denying the natural
sexual rights of the body. And here he was, losing his
grip, his confidence, doubting, guilt trying to close its
shroud over him, to force him to be some kind of
improbable boy-angel, "pure," whatever meaning
that might have. But where? What? Where was he
sure? What fundamentally did he have to hold on to?

Himself.

And just how much of himself was there, and how
solid was it?

Sheer drugged exhaustion forced him into a cloudy
sleep toward dawn.

When he did wake up late next morning and

stepped out onto his balcony, it was to an unaccus-
tomed overcast, lowering sky. Gray gatherings of
heavy clouds had settled over the coast. Maybe it
would even rain. Then another forest fire would become less likely.

"Pray for rain," he said jokingly to Neville as he
carried in his breakfast tray.

His face seemed to stiffen. He set down the tray.
"Monsieur?" he queried as though not understand-
ing.

"Pray for rain. No more forest fires."

Impassive, glancing sideways and down, he murmured again, "Monsieur," in a tone of comprehen-
sion, and withdrew.

They assembled in the living room around eleven
o'clock and because of the weather agreed that it was
a good day to go down into Cannes and do errands.
Mimi was of course going daily to her ballet class,
Xavier had some business at the Town Hall in connection with the marriage permits, Mrs. Lucas
wanted to have her hair done, and Brendan wanted
to wander around alone for a little while.

In the center of town he dropped off the others,
parked the car and began trudging along the Rue
d'Antibes. Then the clouds released the rain. This
was the South; this was summer. Brendan took shelter under a shop awning. The rain cascaded down
over everything, the gutters were swiftly transformed into rushing streams, hurtling water shut
down in an instant the outdoor openness of Cannes,
cleared the streets, swept the café terraces. Un-
believable sheets of water pounded down just in
front of him.

Almost as quickly as it started, it stopped. That should keep any fires from spreading through the hills for a while. He continued along the Rue d'Antibes. There were many girls in long white boots and long black or blond hair loitering with tired seductiveness in doorways. There were four young men in tight pullover sweaters, shirts and tighter pants also loitering there.

The South of France had always exuded sexuality for Brendan. It was in the musky air, the sticky sea, the sensuous food, the sensual wine. It was woven into the bed sheets. Pillows were stuffed with it. All streets, not just this one, were entangled in it. Sex lurked around the churches and hung from the Maritime pines. Storms blew more of it in. It never ebbed with the tide: the Mediterranean had no tide.

And yet here he was, not having any sexual life. He seemed to be waiting breathless for some thunderclap of desire, of opportunity, a sexual epiphany. He did not know from what quarter it would come. But he had a vague inkling that it was in some way intertwined with the marriage, or the separation, of Xavier and Miriam.

Arriving back at his car, he began driving aimlessly around Cannes until it would be time to join the others at the Festival Restaurant for lunch. Cannes, once a typically ramshackle, enchanting Mediterranean fishing village, was disappearing under featureless slabs of glass apartment houses just like every other modern city in the world. These thousands of windows stared blankly out to sea; they glaringly reflected the sun in its daily passage, gushed electricity at night.

Row on row of yachts, all for hire, filled the water-front. Next to the docks the big gambling casino nightly sucked in unsmiling crowds who wanted to lose. Brassy entertainers made the walls of the gro-tesquely expensive night clubs quake. This was vaca-tionland.

He arrived at the Festival, its open front giving a view of the narrow strip of yellow beach and the sea beyond, to find a slim blond girl in a light blue blouse and pants sitting at a corner table with his group; it was Ariane, Xavier's sister. He had always found her charming, all style and sincerity, happily married and with two small children.

"Look who blew in!" exclaimed Xavier gaily.

Ariane, with her back to him, turned with an almost stricken look to see who it was, fearful that she cause hurt feelings by not having the name on the tip of her tongue. Seeing Brendan, relief came into her face. They embraced. "Because of all the sunshine," she giggled, "which I knew you were all basking in down here, I just got on a plane. Henri and the kids are at his mother's this week, so—"

"And just in time," said Xavier. "I *think* I've got all the permits we need."

"Really?" exclaimed Mimi, wide-eyed.

"I think so."

Mrs. Lucas folded and unfolded her napkin.

"That's great," Brendan said, and turning to Ariane, "How did you know we'd be having lunch here?"

"I called your house. A person with a very strange

voice—it sounded as if he were at the bottom of a well—told me. Who is he?"

"The cook."

"Shall we order," said Mrs. Lucas. It was not a question.

CHAPTER
FIVE

F O R   D I N N E R that evening Brendan had invited an American golf professional, Chuck Bellamy,
to join them. From the Festival he telephoned Neville to say that they would be six instead of five for
dinner. Almost inaudibly Neville answered, "I see,"
or something to that effect.

In the afternoon, with the weather steadily clearing, a marvelously fresh and sparkling Mediterranean day superseded the storm. They roamed
around doing different errands, and what with one
thing and another it was six o'clock before they arrived back at the Mas.

The house was perfectly still, baking in the long
rays of the late afternoon sun. It was completely
closed up again, every shutter shut. Brendan thought

Neville must be trying to keep the interior cool. The house in a peculiar way was acquiring changing, suggestive atmospheres to him. Now he suddenly saw in it the sealed aspect of a fastness, as though guarding in its depths something so volatile that no faintest tremor or even breeze must affect the waiting stillness of this big yellowish manse.

The row on row of orange trees, their stunted fruit hanging immobile, preserved an equal stillness.

He honked the horn of the car, in order to get Neville to come down and carry up Ariane's luggage. The sound broke over the mute orchard and house with startling bluntness. When he didn't appear Brendan couldn't bring himself to honk again.

"Xavier and I will take care of them," he said as they all started through the gate and up through the trees.

"Why do you keep it all shut up that way?" inquired Ariane as she strode along beside Brendan.

"I don't. Neville does."

"Neville does so many things on his own," observed his mother from just in front of them.

He glanced back. Xavier and Miriam were coming along more slowly, his hand on her shoulder. It occurred to him that this marriage was the last thing in the world he wanted. And yet he had introduced them, had sheltered their love-making here, and undoubtedly would be the one literally to give her to him in the marriage ceremony. Some inevitability had forced him to assist a romance he now saw was wrong. Xavier was too nervous and too selfish. Brendan had known that. Xavier was wrong for her, wrong for everybody.

They reached the big, windowless front door. It

was locked. Brendan opened it with his key and they entered the dark front hall. There was something curiously wrong there. Even in the dim light he saw what it was. Two fairly large, jagged holes had been ripped in the carpet. He called for Neville. There was no answer. He went left through the archway into the living room. A kitchen chair was overturned in the middle of it. There was some broken glass in a corner. A lamp lay smashed on the floor.

He went through the dining room toward the kitchen calling for Neville. Mimi and Xavier followed. There was no answer.

The kitchen looked as though it had been rifled by a spastic burglar.

Something moved from under the table. Titus, showing the whites of his eyes, tail between his legs, crept out. He made his way to Xavier and sat down very close to his legs, trembling.

Every drawer and cupboard in the kitchen was open. Flour had been spilled all over the place. Pots and pans were everywhere. Two plucked chickens had been wildly slashed and lay with guts exposed, heads half off on the sideboard. Chicken curry was tonight's menu, Brendan recalled automatically. He called Neville's name again. There was no response. Outside the kitchen door the garbage pails were overturned, and refuse—orange peels, eggshells, old food of all kinds—lay scattered about, as though the phantom burglar had been searching there too.

"Have we been robbed?" Mimi murmured apprehensively. And then, for such is the power of suggestion, however far-fetched and rejected at first: "Algerians . . .?"

"Where's Neville?" said Xavier in a flat voice.

"He's not answering," Brendan said. "I'll check his room."

Neville's room was at the other end of the back corridor from the kitchen. But as he started down it Brendan heard a door slam and then Neville was coming toward him from the dim far end of the hall.

He had never noticed before how Neville walked. Perhaps this particular gait of his was new. He walked like some famous woman movie star of the old school, one shoulder then the other coming rather provocatively forward, legs swinging smartly one before the other. A silver fox cape flung over his shoulders would have made the image complete. The grotesqueness of the gait in line with his powerful frame had an unbalancing impact.

"Monsieur," he murmured, going swiftly by Brendan into the kitchen.

Brendan waited a moment, then said a little breathlessly, "What happened?"

He looked around him in apparent quiet bewilderment. "Happened?"

"Why is everything messed up like this?"

"I don't mind."

"I need a drink," murmured Xavier dryly.

"Drink, is it!" cried Neville in a ringing voice, one they would never have suspected he possessed. "Then you'll be wanting ice!" And crossing swiftly to the refrigerator he opened the door, grabbed an ice tray and instantly flung it as hard as possible back over his shoulder. It shot through the open kitchen door and skidded into the spilled garbage.

Miriam whirled and was out of the kitchen in one motion.

"You're drunk!" shouted Xavier.

"I never drank a drop in my life," answered Neville, his voice becoming nasally scornful. "That's for you high-class shits." Then he moved forward and in a louder voice demanded, "Isn't it!"

He turned toward Brendan. The kitchen table was between them. Brendan noticed that the butcher knife and meat cleaver were laid out on it, in an orderly, even ceremonious arrangement, and that amid the chaos of the kitchen this table, with that arrangement, alone was immaculate. "You just think you're high-class," Neville spat at him. "You. *Monsieur.*" The last word was sounded like the beginning of a vomit.

"If you're not drunk"—Brendan was trying to sound calmly authoritative but a tremor was undermining him—"what the hell do you think you're doing?"

A silence. "What am I *doing!*" Neville's hands came to rest on the table as he leaned across it. *"What am I doing!"* He began to move around the table toward Brendan, eyes fixed on his. Brendan realized numbly that he had never looked him in the eye before. "Did you think I wasn't going to protect myself? Did you think I'm some peasant to stand by until you finish me off? Don't you think I know how to protect myself from you others? Haven't I for *years? All these years!* And *still* you come after me!" Neville was close to him, glaring. There was no smell of liquor, no sign of drunkenness.

Xavier stepped up close to Brendan's side. "Go back over to the other side of the room," he murmured to Neville.

They beheld each other, then Neville looked

down, seemed to ponder for a moment, and rather docilely moved back toward the refrigerator.

This kitchen was the arena of his actions, his defiance had to happen here; what kind of sacrifice . . . bread and wine . . . body . . . blood . . . did he plan to offer up from here?

"Brendan!" called Mrs. Lucas, coming through the dining room toward the kitchen. "What's going on in there?"

Sensing that his mother's presence in the kitchen now would be the match to the fuse, Brendan intercepted her in the pantry and turned back with her toward the living room. Xavier followed, Mrs. Lucas craning her neck to see past them. "What on earth—" she began.

"He lost something," Brendan said, "and got upset."

He herded her back into the living room with Ariane and Mimi. Xavier and he exchanged a taut, surmising look. On their way upstairs he whispered tensely to Xavier, "What in God's name are we going to do? How can we phone the police with the only phone in the kitchen! Why don't you go for them?"

"We can't get the police. Not yet. He hasn't really done anything. Maybe he'll calm down," he added, though in an unconvinced tone, "maybe *tout s'arrangera.*"

It was a very French attitude. They believed that about most problems, and apparently it was true for them. But Neville wasn't French.

Dressed for dinner, Brendan came down to find his mother, Miriam, Ariane and Chuck Bellamy sitting

on the terrace having drinks. They made a singularly
attractive group in this setting, with the orchard glis-
tening below them, Cannes and then the sea
dramatically spread beyond and below, and themselves arranged in a semicircle on the geranium-bor-
dered terrace, the long mellow evening light playing
on Ariane's blond hair and light blue dress, Miriam's
stylishness in pink, his mother upright and distin-
guished-looking in a long flowered gown, and Chuck
Bellamy, bursting with reddish health, in a madras
jacket and yellow slacks. They looked so well-fed and
well-dressed and above all secure, up here above the
coast, surrounded by their stone house and their
trees and money, healthy beings all, waiting for dinner to be served.

The piny jasmine fumes of the hills wove around
them, promising and insinuating, a loosening spirit
pervading always the South of France.

"Well, Bennie," exclaimed Chuck, springing up to
throw an arm around his shoulders, "quite a spread
you got here!" Brendan's nickname was Denny to
everybody but Chuck. He'd always meant to mention that to him. "Let me see the view from over
here," and Chuck led him to the far end of the terrace. "Who's the chick? Boy!"

"That's Ariane, Xavier's sister. Happily married.
Two children."

"Boy," he repeated, not seeming to have heard the
last two of the three facts told him.

Neville, in his white jacket, came onto the terrace
carrying a tray with Brendan's usual drink, bourbon
and water. As Xavier had said, You can take the boy
out of the South, but you can't take the bourbon out
of the boy. Neville came up to Brendan, eyes on the

ground, and he looked as normal as he ever looked, except that he seemed to list slightly to the left and his coloring was a little more sallow. As Brendan watched him, his eyes slid sideways to his mother, who was staring in front of her. Then they slid back and he turned and left the terrace.

"Where'd you get the butler?" asked Chuck. "Out of some murder novel?"

Brendan tried to chuckle.

"He's the one that did it, all right. What a face."

Crude in a way though he was, Chuck had his own shrewdness. The reassurance Neville's return to routine behavior had given Brendan evaporated.

Xavier did not appear. Finally Brendan went up to see what was detaining him. He found him in his shower. His bedroom and the adjoining bedroom had become a Turkish bath in atmosphere. Finding his way to the shower curtain he yelled, "What are you trying to do? Melt yourself down?"

Xavier's drenched head emerged. "I'll be right out." Brendan had the sudden perception that he would have stayed in there for days if necessary until someone came to escort him to dryness. It was warm in the shower stall, warm and enclosing and protecting. Brendan moved into the bedroom and opened a window. Gradually the steam dissipated. Xavier came in, slowly drying his long frame. "I feel better," he said.

"Didn't you feel well before?"

He lay down on the bed and began methodically drying his feet.

"Come and have a drink." Brendan started to leave.

"Ah—did your guest arrive?"

"Yes."

"Ah—do you mind—keeping me company while I get dressed? I'm sort of, well, *spooked* right now."

"Yes, of course. I'm sort of spooked, too. Right now he's calm. I should have known from all his paranoid stories that something like this might happen."

"Lots of people tell crazy stories. Not too many lay out the meat cleaver."

"Mmm, the meat cleaver."

"Well," sighed Xavier philosophically, "I guess we'll just see."

When Xavier had finished dressing they went down and joined the others on the terrace. Evening was slowly fading in over them, and over their isolated house in the woods.

"Is that smoke?" asked Ariane. "It looks like a column of smoke up there on top of that hill back there."

"Oh no," Brendan muttered.

"Maybe I'm imagining it," she put in. "Hard to be sure in this twilight."

"It's smoke, miss," said Neville, coming through the door with a drink for Xavier. "We're having a little return of an earlier forest fire."

Mimi's hand trembled as she reached for a piece of cheese. "Maybe we should move," she said in a low voice. "To a hotel in Cannes. Just for tonight. To be on the safe side."

Neville said, "I've checked with the authorities. After all that rain this morning they said it can't amount to much."

Mimi sat still. Neville crossed the stone terrace to the house. Chuck said heartily, "How about doing a little gambling tonight? The Cannes casino—"

"I think we already are," murmured Xavier.

"—has some great entertainment, too, somebody told me. What's that French singer's name . . . Bidet, Bidot, something like that."

"Bécaud," put in Ariane. "Gilbert Bécaud."

"That's the guy."

"Do you like him?"

"Oh yeah. He's great."

"He writes some of his own songs," added Ariane.

"That's what I like about you French. I knew *you* were French as soon as I set eyes on you, because of your beautiful style. You French have got lots of different talents. Now, who ever heard of Frank Sinatra writing his own songs?"

"The Beatles do," put in Mimi.

"They're English."

"Well—"

"Monsieur," said Neville from the doorway, "may I speak to you in private?"

Brendan looked across at him, wondering what he should do.

"What is it?" said Xavier evenly, fixing his eyes on Neville. "Why do you want to see Mr. Lucas?"

Never taking his gaze from Brendan's face Neville said, "In the kitchen, please, monsieur."

"And the English," went on Chuck robustly, "are Europeans, just like the French. See what I mean?"

"Monsieur," said Neville evenly from the doorway.

Suddenly Brendan saw himself in the role of a dog being summoned. Next he might be whistled for. The hell with Neville. This was his house.

He got up. Neville turned on his heel and he fol-

lowed him across the living room, through the dining
room and on—because he did not want the others to
hear what would be said—through the pantry and
into the kitchen.

Neville briskly shut the door behind him and
locked it. The door leading to the outside was already
shut, and locked. The door leading to the back hall
was also shut and locked. All the inside doors of the
Mas Tranquilitat had locks on them. The house was
as though fortified from assaults from the outside and
also uprisings within.

The kitchen had been partially straightened up.
The big oval kitchen table still held the butcher knife
and meat cleaver.

"What is it you want?" Brendan heard himself say.

From the other side of the table Neville cried out,
"That woman, that mother, went through my room,
through my things. Searched everything. She wants
to find evidence," his rage was gathering strength,
"she wants to trap me. It's a trap you're all setting for
me!"

And so I walked into yours, Brendan reflected with
a vagrant foreboding. He knew Neville was telling
the truth about his room being searched, and he
knew his instinct that it had been Mrs. Lucas was
accurate. Of course she would have to go through his
room: her will be done.

The situation here remained too dangerous for
Brendan to show or even really feel fear. "There's
no trap here. If Mother looked into your room it wa
. . . it wa . . ."—Oh God, no stuttering—"it was just
to see that you were comfortable." His stammer had
apparently not passed unnoticed.

"Who else have you trapped? You work all over the world, don't you? Jordan and all those places. It's easy to dispose of people in Jordan and all those places. Bury them in the sand in the desert up to their necks and then pour honey over their heads and leave the rest to the ants and the vultures. Huh!" He began to move toward Brendan. "Huh!"

His head haloed in unreality, Brendan heard an echoing version of his voice say with seeming calm, "There's no plot and there's no trap. Now I'm going back to my guests."

"You're not leaving here! Monsieur!" He spat out the word. "I'm going to get that *mother* of yours in here and I'll chop her up like *one of those chickens!* I'll stretch her neck just like I do a chicken's! *Do you hear me!* I'll take care of the *houseful* of you! You're all involved! All of you! Look out. Huh. Look out. One by one. My knife. One by one. Or. All together. Huh? You take—"

There was a sharp rapping on the back corridor door. "Denny? Open the door." Xavier sounded very authoritative. "Neville! Open this door instantly!"

"Don't move," said Neville.

"There are laws in this country," said Xavier in a warning tone. "If you don't open the door, Neville, the country will be pursuing you, all of us, you'll never escape."

"What do I care!" he said wildly. But it was not convincing.

"Open this door," ordered Xavier in the same authoritative manner. "Then all will be all right. No problems."

Neville sucked in some air noisily and then,

becoming the other Neville, said in his nasal tone, "Oh monsieur, I wanted everything to be so perfect for you."

Brendan swiftly unlocked the door and stepped into the hall. From there he and Xavier beheld Neville, turned in upon himself once again, the always-working, too-perfect servant. He twisted a dishtowel one way then the other in his big hands. "Dinner will be ready in half an hour, monsieur," he murmured and hurried back to the sink.

Xavier and Brendan drifted back toward the terrace. "Did you hear him raving?" he demanded in a low voice. Xavier nodded. "What are we going to do?"

"Search me. It beats me, it just beats me." He shook his head in bewilderment. "The only telephone is in the kitchen. If we call someone—the police or someone—he's sure to hear us. Then he could *really* go berserk."

"There are three men here. And also three able-bodied women. And one Neville."

"You have a gun, or anything?"

He shook his head grimly. He had always been armed in Jordan, like everybody else. But a gun, here, in the sunny, laughing South of France? Only paranoids, only people who thought Algerians were going to break in and butcher them, would have guns here.

"Well," Xavier tried for a calm, studied tone of voice, "Neville has got a butcher knife and a meat cleaver, and who knows what else."

"And then he's crazy. That's a weapon, too."

"So," Xavier looked cogitatively up at the ceiling, as though working out a conundrum, "it might be—

well, very messy if we tried to, you know, subdue him by force. He is strong."

"What shall we do?"

"He seems calm enough now."

"Pour l'instant, as you Frogs say." Brendan chortled erratically.

"I suppose the thing to do would be to go through with dinner, and then—well . . ."

"And then—well . . ."

"And then . . ."

It seemed that both of them considered inaction the best form of action. Reaching around inside, that was what Brendan seemed to find left to do: nothing.

They stepped out on the terrace.

"What's going on in there?" queried Mrs. Lucas, sitting like a relaxing sovereign in her armchair in her long flowered garden-party-at-Buckingham-Palace gown.

"Cook's very upset," Brendan said shortly, his anger at her rising, at this battering ram of a woman who lacked the essential attribute of a woman: intuition. She never had a notion of what those around her were feeling, especially if they were her own flesh and blood. "He's very upset," he had to go on, his voice hardening, "by what happened to his room. It's been gone through."

She shifted her position in the chair. "Gone through. Not exactly. Tidied up. I did straighten it up for him a bit. For such a neat-looking man he does live in such disorder!"

"But Mother," he protested in exasperation, "you saw how much he was going to resent that! You knew it!"

"Resent it! He's not in a position to resent supervision by his employers."

"*I'm* his employer and I didn't *want* that supervision!"

Her face set. He watched her mind switching to the Nice-to-Washington airline schedules.

Mimi put in, "When we've all had one of his good dinners we'll all feel better, especially Neville." But her glance to Brendan said, Do we dare stay for it?

Chuck Bellamy said, "I don't know, European performers just have more class than those hicks and junkies who try to entertain us back home. Take Edith Piaf. Now, there was a great star."

After a silence someone wearily offered, "Judy Garland . . ."

"Judy Garland wasn't in it with Edith Piaf. Like, I tour a lot—well, almost all the time—on the golf circuit, and I'm not doing too bad, either. Last year— let's see, last year I think in prize money I grossed around eighty-seven five. Not bad for waving your arms around in the air, right?"

Xavier murmured, "May I speak to you a minute, darling?" He led Mimi to the end of the terrace and whispered to her. She came back with her eyes flashing fear. Then he beckoned to his sister. After their low-voiced conference Ariane returned to her chair with a thoughtful, concentrated look on her face.

"I don't know," went on Chuck, sloshing more vodka into his glass from the tray Neville had left on the terrace, "sometimes I think I could play better golf if I had a better gallery. American audiences, they get what they deserve. They don't know *how* to appreciate star quality like the people over here do. What do you think?" he said to Brendan.

Brendan had been tracing a blood vessel across his temple with his left hand. "Hm? Oh. I—well, I guess so, yes."

"Not listening, are you, buddy boy?"

"Oh yeah, yes. It's just the cook problem . . ."

"Well, I guess if you're a professional you have to deliver your best no matter how much is against you. Now take the time I was playing in Atlanta . . ."

Brendan's hearing closed down on Chuck Bellamy because of less insistent but far more significant noises coming from the interior of the house.

A door slammed violently on the ground floor, then another upstairs. Lights flashed erratically on and off. Then he saw Neville swiftly cross the living room and kick savagely at a chair in his path. On the rampage, he careened through the house.

As they all sat still, except for Chuck whose monologue continued, Mrs. Lucas interposed in her most even tone: "What are you going to do?"

Brendan drew a long breath; it made him light-headed for a second. "I'll go and see about it," he said, heaving himself out of his chair and heading for the kitchen. But this time he instinctively went by the outdoor route, through the orchard. In his psyche the Mas Tranquilitat had now passed into Neville's control, Neville of the knife and the cleaver and the locks and the knowledge of the cellar and prior occupancy.

So he went around the outside of the house, or, more accurately, crept around it, and stealthily peered in through a kitchen window. Neville was back in the kitchen and again seemed to be preparing a meal.

He crept back around his house to the others on

the terrace. "Temper tantrum," he said. "All right now."

It grew later and darker. Darkness was the ally of what was dark within Neville, what would flourish in the dark. As the lights began to go out in many of the hotel windows and villas and apartments in Cannes, as people went to bed and the prevailing nighttime spirit deepened and spread, civilization and sanity began their nightly shrinkage and withdrawal, and the world became more and more the domain of the criminal and the evil and the ill. Brendan knew they would have to do something soon, or they would be alone in this isolated house in a dead nighttime world with a rampaging psychotic whose illness, he was sure, would deepen and grow in the black atmosphere it needed.

"We'd better eat if we're even going to," said Mimi. "Personally I never was less hungry in my life."

"You dancers eat like little birds, don't you," said Chuck cozily.

"Mmm," she murmured, gazing into the middle distance.

"Why don't we go and see—" began Xavier, when Neville appeared in the doorway, white-jacketed, a towel over his arm, more formal than ever. "Dinner," he said in his metallic way, staring over their heads, "is served."

They trailed in through the living room murmuring to each other. The dining room table had been set in the usual way, the only difference being that instead of the electric chandelier they were dining tonight by candlelight—two in the middle of the ta-

ble in their silver candlesticks, two in the wall
sconces. The light brought an orange hue out in the
walls, as though a reflection of the fruit on the trees
outdoors, and shed a glow of spurious romanticism
over the room.

The meal seemed a ritual, the breaking of bread,
as at a Last Supper. While Neville circled around
behind them with the platter of chicken, serving fork
and butcher knife, they went through with this
nerve-racking charade out of an atavistic sense of
bread-breaking and its central place in a sane, civilized life. *Give us this day . . . as we forgive those who
trespass against us . . .*

"Will you say grace?" said Mrs. Lucas suddenly to
Brendan from the other end of the table.

He was taken completely by surprise; he hadn't
thought of grace in years. Lowering his head,
he murmured, "Bless us O Lord and these Thy
gifts . . ."

Mass, holiness, prayer, ritual—all now inextricably
tangled with candles and knives and plots, smoke in
the hills, poisonous trees: something deranged loose
all around them, as uncontainable as an epidemic.

"You may serve now, Neville," he heard his
mother say.

Xavier and Mimi had the chairs on the side of the
table next to the sideboard and the wall. Xavier
perched on his chair like a runner about to hear the
starting gun; Mimi too seemed ready at any moment
to spring up and fly away. Mrs. Lucas sat at the far
end calmly, turning a fork slowly with her left hand
as though checking it for absolute cleanliness. Opposite Xavier and Mimi, Chuck and Ariane sat with

their backs to the living room, Chuck easing into
drunkenness, Ariane very self-contained and
thoughtful-looking—a lovely vision in her blondness
by candlelight. Her adoring husband and two adoring children were in the North, visiting his mother;
perhaps they were sitting down to their dinner and
had just said grace, too.

Neville passed behind her carrying a large platter
of dismembered chicken, with the fork and knife,
and brought it to Brendan to serve himself first.
Brendan realized that this was an attempt to insult
his mother, but he said nothing, and helped himself
from the platter.

Then Neville proceeded around the table and
seemed to be performing as usual, except that the
strange listing of his posture persisted, and except
that everyone at the table with the apparent omis-
sion of Chuck and Mrs. Lucas knew the extremity of
his inner rage.

Chuck had come to enjoy himself and he was simply brushing aside and drinking away anything and
everything that stood in the way of that. His pleasant
evening was not to be interfered with. Presumably if
the house now exploded he would take notice of that,
but not of anything else.

Mrs. Lucas had no intuition but she was very alert
and observant, and Brendan suspected that she
sensed much of what was transpiring. If so, that
would make her calm self-possession something to
admire.

Unlike all of Neville's work up to this time, the
chicken had been very clumsily cut up and its innards not cleaned out, so that the guts and waste

were still there in bits and pieces; it was also under-
cooked, cold. Then he served some cold, milky
mashed potatoes. A dank salad followed. Brendan
was sure it was all deliberate: with this bad food he
was insulting everybody. Take this, he was saying, it's
fit for swine.

Fear now closed more tightly than ever around
Brendan's head. Neville's presenting them with this
mess revealed a rage in the cook even more violent,
more ultimate than he'd imagined. It did violence to
the one area of self-pride he possessed: his skill as a
chef. It was self-lacerating. He was figuratively beating his head against the wall. This sorry parade of
dishes meant that Neville had no control of himself
left, that there was now no self. There was only rage.

Suddenly Xavier snapped upright in his chair.
"Where's my dog!" he demanded of the table.

They all looked at each other and Mimi said she'd
seen Titus taking a nap under the dining room table
before they all went out for drinks on the terrace.
Futilely, Xavier looked under the table and the sideboard. "Neville," he then said quietly and clearly,
"have you seen my dog?"

"That dog?" said Neville in his tinlike tone. "No."
He went out into the kitchen.

"He's done something to my dog!" said Xavier in
a tone of low-pitched violence.

"There's no reason at all to think that," said Ariane
in the pleasantest tone her smooth, musical voice
possessed. "Titus is probably out in the trees somewhere."

"I'm going to look for him," said Xavier, slamming
his napkin onto the table.

"I'm coming too," cried Mimi.

They disappeared out to the terrace.

Neville came in. "We'll have coffee on the ter-race," said Mrs. Lucas.

"And what about Monsieur the Count and Miss Lucas?"

"They've gone to search for the dog," Brendan said, and he looked into Neville's colorless eyes. Did he imagine the reflection of several chancy emotions, or did he see it?

They moved out onto the terrace, under the great spread of a starry Mediterranean sky. Fewer lights than ever remained burning in Cannes below them. For a world-renowned resort at the height of the season, Cannes seemed to have the early-to-bed hab-its of a boy scout camp. Whom could they rouse if they had to? Who would come to their aid? Who was on duty? Where?

Mrs. Lucas led Brendan to the end of the terrace. "I think your cook is either insane or going insane," she said quietly. "You're aware of that."

"I know. The question is, what are we going to do about it?"

"Call the authorities, of course."

"The only phone in this cheapskate's house is in the kitchen. He'd hear us. And then I'm sure he'd turn completely violent. Mother. I think I have to tell you this." He touched her arm to reassure her. "He's threatening you personally. For going through his room. He thinks it's all a big plot against him and you're the ringleader."

She turned to look at him closely. "I'm not fright-ened by threats," she said. "When I was younger, like

these girls here, I would have been absolutely terrified, of course. But then I had not had my life
. . . your father . . . you children . . . I've had my life,
or most of it . . . threats . . ." Her voice trailed off.

She was telling the truth. So that was what growing
old meant: life, for her at least, lessening in value.

As for himself, standing now in the darkness with
a murderous man loose and armed and threatening
him and all of them, Brendan knew that he would
not, could not, surrender his life. I am unkillable, he
thought: if Neville stabbed me in the heart I would
return as a ghost; if they buried me I would rise from
the grave; if cremated, I would become the phoenix.
He felt irresistibly alive; his resources had hardly
been tapped and could not be quenched, not now. At
his mother's age, probably, but not now.

"He's just a poor sick boy," she went on. "Poor
wretched sick boy."

"And very dangerous."

"What are we going to do?"

She, too, asked the ultimate question. The situation
seemed a dead-end street, and all of them were led
up sooner or later, neurotically and fearfully or
calmly and rationally, to this blank wall: What are we
going to do?

In the distance, from here and there, faintly over
the hills they sometimes could hear Xavier's voice.
"Titus! . . . Titus! . . ."

Neville came out on the terrace with a tray of little
cups and a coffeepot. With the rigidity of an automa-
ton he poured for the rest of them. They took their
cups and sat down. After he left Brendan said edgily,
"It's getting later, later and later."

"He seems better now," put in Ariane.

"It comes in waves," Brendan said, "in pulsations, like a fever. The next one is going to be bigger than the last one . . ."

She sat, neck straight, hands folded in her lap, eyes lowered, like a convent girl who is being perfect and so immune to reprimand.

"This coffee is one thing the French are nowhere with," observed Chuck Bellamy. "Boy. What I wouldn't give for some Maxwell House!"

"Chuck," Brendan said. He looked at him. "Why don't you go into the kitchen and tell Neville about that?"

"Should I!"

He looked steadily at him. "Yes. I think you should. Maybe he can make a better cup if he really tries."

Chuck moved off the terrace, leaving Brendan to nurse his thoughts and his fears. He was not so much afraid of physical attack by Neville; it was very possible and Neville was bigger and a fanatic, but until it happened that possibility remained abstract in his imagination, as though it were a movie he might or might not see. He could not feel it, having no prior experience to base any feeling on.

What he did have instinctive knowledge of, in his bones, in his brain, was that madness was contagious, suspicion bred suspicion, paranoia bred paranoia, and he knew that he was by no means immune.

Madness: the most contagious disease in the world.

Chuck reached the closed kitchen door. "Hi there!" he called out, bursting through.

Neville was standing with his back to him on the

near side of the kitchen table, resting his large hands on it. The meat cleaver and the butcher knife were still in place. He started at this sudden eruption into his sanctuary and cried out in a high, strangled voice, "What do you want! What are you doing here! Get out!"

Chuck stopped short. Then resuming his big grin he advanced a step. "Listen, friend, I just wanted to see your layout here. Hmm. Nice layout. Too bad you can't turn out better *food!* Ha. No offense. About that coffee—well, you got any 'instant'? You know, instant Maxwell House or something like that? American?"

Neville had been slowly rotating his torso away from facing the table to facing Chuck. In a low voice he said, "I don't let cheap Americans in here."

"You . . . you . . . ha, what was that?"

"Who invited you to this house?"

"Who *invited* me? What do you mean, who invited me? What's going on around here, anyway? If it hadn't been for the vodka I couldn't have stuck with this lousy dinner, I—"

"Lousy, was it?"

"Yah, lousy food, creepy atmosphere—"

"Did *she* invite you, or did Monsieur?"

"She? Mother Lucas? Naw. Bennie asked me. It's his house."

An indeterminate silence and expression settled over Neville at these words.

Chuck went on. "I never met the old lady before."

". . . never will again . . ."

"Huh? What?"

". . . never again . . ."

The intensity of his tone cut into Chuck's dulled

consciousness. He took a cleared look at Neville's face. "I . . . ah . . . never will? Why won't I?"

Neville slid sideways and moved to get behind his table. "Are you an investigator?"

"What do you mean? What investigator?"

"Why did you come here to question me?" demanded Neville peremptorily.

"Ah . . ." Chuck began, his voice turning suddenly tentative. "The coffee, ah—"

"The coffee! I'll get you some coffee!" cried Neville, heading toward the stove.

"No, no, never . . . I . . . no coffee—well, I'll just go back now to the terrace—"

"Tell *them,*" cried Neville in a voice which rooted Chuck to the spot, "YOU TELL THEM I'M GOING TO STRETCH THEIR NECKS LIKE THOSE CHICKENS WERE . . . YOU TELL THEM I'LL CUT THEIR INSIDES INTO SHREDS . . . YOU TELL *HER* THAT HER EYES ARE GOING TO GET TORN OUT, WITH THIS!" He snatched up the butcher knife and then said, his voice falling deep into his chest, "Got that! Mr. Investigator!" Chuck, as though in slow motion, made a move toward the door. "You, Mr. Investigator. Yes. You too. You're fat! You, you need my cleaver. The knife or the cleaver, for all of you scum."

Moving slowly, as though through water, Chuck was able to gain the door and pass beyond it into the other room.

Lurching onto the terrace, Chuck looked as though he had been kicked in the stomach. His ruddy color had turned to an unhealthy flush; his eyes were still blurred with drinking but now stared in befuddled astonishment.

"The guy is nuts!" he rasped. "He's not dealing with a full deck!" He turned from one to the other of them. "What are you going to do?"

The question. But this time it carried the Chuck Bellamy variation: not What are we going to do? but What are *you* going to do?

Brendan went up close to him. "What did he say?"

"What did he say! He wants to butcher us all, that's what he said!"

"Yes, well," said Brendan quietly, "then he hasn't changed his lines."

Chuck gaped at him. "You mean he said that *before?*" Brendan nodded. "And *still* you sent me in there! *Alone!* Nice guy! Nice pal!"

Brendan looked at him. "It was the only way I could think of to catch your attention. I couldn't seem to make you *notice* that our lives are in danger. Well, now you know. They are. We've got to stick together. We need all the help we can get. You've got to help us."

Chuck cocked his reddish head at him; the eyes tightened, became less groggy. He sobered himself up in an instant there in front of them.

"Me?" he said in an undertone using his wise-guy voice, frowning, tough, Look-Out-Fer-Number-One Chuck. "What could I do?" He went over to Ariane. "Now then," he said, taking one of her hands, "you're not getting cold feet are you? Or cold hands?"

She was so attractive that even the fixed, negative smile she turned on for him illuminated her face. "I wonder where my brother is," she said, turning away and frowning. "What can they hope to find wandering around in the dark like that?"

"They both took flashlights," said Mrs. Lucas. "And

of course like all shepherds the dog has marvelous
hearing."

"If he can still hear anything," Brendan said com-
pulsively, with no prior notion he was going to say it.

"What d'ya mean?" said Chuck. "What could happen to a dog up here? There's no traffic for him to get
run over. What could happen?"

"Mrs. Lucas," said Neville from the doorway,
"come with me to the kitchen." It was a steely order,
such as a member of that world-girdling conspiracy
pursuing him might have issued. From being pur-
sued by Them he had transformed himself into one
of their number.

Mrs. Lucas looked up at him analytically from her
chair. "Certainly not," she said.

It was then that Brendan saw part of the knife
shining beneath the towel Neville had over his right
hand.

"Don't lie to me!" he cried, his voice rising. "I
know who you are!"

"Don't raise your voice," she said. She looked at
him. "What do you mean by making these scenes?
What kind of training did you have?"

"What kind of training! What do you—tricks! I
see . . ." His face was becoming distorted, the muscles
pulling it unnaturally this way and that. "Now I'm
stopping all tricks! All plots. Now. The kitchen."

"Neville." Brendan got out of his chair. "Put that
knife away. No. Give me that knife." Mrs. Lucas and
Ariane both were suddenly very shaken, not having
seen or suspected the knife; Chuck swayed slightly
on the balls of his feet. "There are four of us and we
are all healthy. If you cut one, the others will get you.
You will be in prison for years. Assault with attempt

to kill. Then you'll really be in the trap you're always
imagining is set for you. You will throw yourself into
it. Give me the knife."

There was a long, piercing silence. Neville, mo-
tionless, gazed at him.

"Then it'll all be over," Brendan went on in as
controlled a voice as possible.

Neville pivoted slowly in his direction.

"We won't say anything about this, to anyone."

Neville stared unwaveringly at him, as though to
extract some absolute guarantee, or renunciation, or
commitment. In some way Brendan and not his
mother was the hub of Neville's encompassing obsession with this family.

"I promise to say nothing . . . on my word as . . . as
a . . ."—American? *Diplomat!*—". . . a Catholic."

Neville was standing in a rather impressive way,
drawn up to his full height, no longer listing, standing
in some kind of dignity born of suffering. He seemed
to be turning over the words in his mind. Brendan
seemed to have gotten through all the distorting
chemistry of his brain to what was left of his reason.
Finally he said in a deeper voice, "Blood is thicker
than love. Yours is anyway. And I wanted . . . things
. . . you . . . but. Blood is thicker. I know that now.
Siding with her." Then very briskly, "Come along,"
to Mrs. Lucas.

She looked unflinchingly up at him. "You have my
son's word as a Catholic. Now surrender that knife.
The whole episode will be forgotten. You've worked
on the Riviera for years. Do you want to throw all
that away—because someone had the consideration
to straighten out your room!"

This allusion seemed a mistake. Color flooded into

his sallow face. "Plotting! Laying a trap!"

But once again the fanaticism was receding in him. Brendan heard it begin to drift out of his voice. The other pulsation, toward some vestigial self-control, was trying to reassert itself. If no one of them made the slightest wrong move, they were going to get past this crisis. Indecisive, Neville stood among them.

Disturbingly, as Brendan looked at Neville at bay, he could all too easily feel his way into his shoes. He was, with that butcher knife in his hand, in command of this house, of them. The "perfect servant," years of resentment decaying his heart, suddenly supreme. The exhilaration of it must have been almost overwhelming him.

"Put the knife down on the table," Brendan murmured to him.

Neville stood immobile with that odd dignity.

"There's no plot against you," Brendan went on, "but if you're unhappy with us—"

He flashed a look at him. "I'm not!" he said hoarsely. "Or I wasn't. I was ha—happy . . . happy . . ."

"Well, then why ruin everything over a misunderstanding? We can go on as before, if you like, as if nothing had hap—well, nothing *has* happened really, and we must make sure it doesn't. Neville." Another quick look at Brendan when he heard his name. Brendan was sensing intimations about something in relation to himself. "We will go on as before, and be . . . happy."

God forbid, Brendan thought, if I get us all out of this alive, that Neville would spend another night under this roof. He was trying to inveigle him into surrendering the knife, and then get the police.

The illusory trap was now real.

"Well," Neville said in his now docile voice, "if that's the way you think about it."

"That is, Neville."

And so his murderous resolve against them slowly, more slowly than ever this time, was receding. Brendan didn't dare breathe or move.

Without putting the knife down, but folding the towel neatly over his arm and hand to conceal it, Neville withdrew into the kitchen.

"This is monstrous," said Mrs. Lucas.

"He's so *ill!*" whispered Ariane.

"That was a close one," said Chuck.

Brendan pulled him a little aside. "Too close. Back there in the kitchen a few minutes from now he'll start remembering all our 'plots' again, all the 'injustices,' fueling himself one more time. The next time," he said shakily, "nobody will be able to talk him out of it."

"How can you be so sure," said Ariane, who had overheard.

He looked at her expressionlessly, then said, "Because I understand how minds like that work."

She said nothing.

In the horror of the butcher knife and the latest confrontation Brendan had completely forgotten about Xavier and Mimi. Xavier might be unstable but he was not crazy—he had escaped from the house—and now they heard a car roaring down the road beside the house and coming to a stop at the gate. Flashlights made their way up through the trees toward us. "Hello!" called out Xavier. "Is everything all right? Hello!"

"Yes," Brendan called back, standing on the terrace. "Who's that with you?"

"The police!" he answered crisply, as he and Mimi came up the steps. Three French policemen followed them onto the terrace and stood there, grouped indecisively.

"He's in the kitchen," Brendan said to them in a low, hurried voice, "the one you want to arrest."

"Arrest?" said the policeman who seemed to be the spokesman. "I don't think this is even our jurisdiction. We can't arrest anybody here. This is Le Cannet territory and our authority is only in the town of Mouguin."

"This *is* Mouguin," Brendan hissed, "and there is an insane man in the kitchen threatening to kill us!"

"Has anybody been injured?"

Brendan gaped at him. "No! Does anybody have to be? Do we have to give you a corpse before you'll act?"

"Don't get nervous, monsieur. Is he armed?"

"Yes. With a butcher knife."

The three policemen visibly blanched at this news, and then very gingerly, each morally supporting the other, edged across the terrace and through the living room. Xavier and Brendan followed. At the closed kitchen door the policemen stepped back, indicating that Brendan should usher them through. He tried the door; it was unlocked and he opened it.

The kitchen was in immaculate condition. Neville was on his knees, scrubbing the floor. He looked up at them questioningly. Until then, the sight of a uniform anywhere in the South of France had thrown him into extreme states of anxiety. Now three uniformed policemen in his kitchen elicited no external reaction at all.

"Monsieur?" he inquired of Brendan.

"Neville, these men want to talk to you."

He got up and wiped his hands on his waist apron.

"What do you want me to say to him?" the spokesman inquired of Brendan dryly in French. "Good evening?"

Flummoxed and enraged, trapped himself, Brendan said in the fastest French he could manage, hoping Neville would not understand, "I want you to arrest him. He's dangerous and sick."

"He doesn't have the look of that." And then, because Brendan was glaring at him so intensely, as was Xavier over his shoulder, the policeman felt he had to make some semblance of performing his duty. "What have you been doing this evening, monsieur?" he said slowly in French to Neville. "You've upset these people here."

"Why . . . nothing," replied Neville in English, widening his eyes. "Preparing dinner. Serving dinner. Straightening up the kitchen."

"Listen, Officer," said Xavier in his most authoritative French, "this man has been menacing our lives here for hours. He threatened Monsieur Lucas's mother with a butcher knife. He is insane, he is criminally insane. He . . . he . . . ." Xavier's excellent authority suddenly began to fall apart, but for a reason that shocked and reinforced. "He poisoned my German shepherd."

"He did!" Brendan exclaimed.

"Can you prove that?" demanded the policeman. "Destruction of personal property." This was serious;

French law could not tolerate that. "How much was the dog worth?"

"Plenty. And yes I can prove it, eventually. Not this instant."

"Monsieur," wailed Neville, coming up to the three of them standing in the doorway. "I didn't, I wouldn't—"

"I found the dog," said Xavier in a dangerous monotone, "dead from poisoning in the woods over there. You had all that arsenic. I'm sure tomorrow when it's light I'll find a piece of meat near him covered with arsenic."

Neville, looking blank, was silent.

"We can't take any action on the mere fact that you found your dog dead," observed the policeman with an attitude of complacent pleasure.

Leading the spokesman back into the dining room, Brendan said to him, "That cook is potentially a murderer. He's dangerous. He menaced our lives over and over. What are you going to do about it?"

The policeman looked at him with his protruding eyes, his mouth set under his black mustache. "He has not broken any law. He has done nothing. Doubtless he had drunk too much, but now he is evidently completely sober. He does not even smell of drink. *I* covertly tested him on that." He cocked an eye at him for his approval of this act of detection, meeting an opaque stare. "After all, monsieur," he went on in a man-to-man tone, "you have two arms. If there is trouble—why, then defend yourself!"

A gleam of rage erupted in the center of Brendan's brain. He had felt nothing remotely like it before in his life. Leveling his eyes on the officer, he said in a

tone so cold it alarmed even him, "Oh, I see. I had
the impression that this was a civilized country here.
Being threatened I turned to the state to help me
and my family. But this is the jungle here. All right.
I understand its laws." He pointed an index finger at
the policeman's face. "Now. I want you three in-
dividuals to get out of here."

The bulbous eyes rolled up and down him.

In that moment Brendan was capable of, and prepared to, kill another human being. It would be self-
defense and defense of his family and nothing was
clearer to him than that he would and could do it.
The policeman had ignited an atavistic layer in his
brain and it sprang instantly alive.

"Look here, monsieur," said the policeman. "We
could take your cook to a hotel until he is more
calm."

"That won't do any good. He'll come right back,
sneak up on us." He had almost discounted any offi-
cial action, but in one last attempt he said, "Will you
put him in jail, tonight?"

"Ah, monsieur, I cannot do that. No charges."

Turning away he then said curtly, "In that case, get
out of my house."

The policeman swung his night stick back and
forth beside his leg for a few moments, gave that
French sigh of resignation to human frailty, and
called out, "Eh, Jean Patrice, Arnaud! Let's go."

Xavier tried to stop them, to reason with them, but
the last traces of reason had escaped from the Mas
Tranquilitat and the three arms of the law, stalwarts
of the *Code Napoléon,* shambled through the orchard and left them.

No one suggested leaving under their protection. Brendan didn't know why none of the others did. For himself, surmounting this menace had become an ordeal too all-involving, too meaningful, to avoid. And they were, after all, three men and three women against one lone individual.

CHAPTER
SIX

"I'VE GOT a knife," Xavier said to Brendan. "The butcher was still open when I drove down to get the police and they lent me this." From inside his jacket he pulled out a blade just as formidable and deadly as Neville's. Brendan drew in a long, mortal breath. The weapons had now been chosen. "Those police," Xavier continued in disgust, "maybe we can sue them—"

"Forget the police. He told me I had two arms to defend myself. That's it."

"There are *three* men here. We have six arms. And three women. In France in the Revolution the women fought on the barricades."

They went into the living room. The women were

sitting agitatedly, desperately together.

"Where's Chuck?" Brendan inquired.

Ariane said, "I saw him go down through the trees just after the police left. Then I . . . thought I heard the lower gate open . . . and shut."

He glanced at Xavier. Chuck would be halfway to Cannes by now. *His* life was not immediately threatened, so he wasn't interested. "We have four arms," he muttered.

"Aux barricades!" exclaimed Xavier with sudden bravado, his eyes sweeping over the women. They looked back at him in puzzlement.

"Where is the cook?" asked Mrs. Lucas. Somehow referring to Neville as "the cook" indicated her indomitability. Mrs. Lucas was going to maintain a view of things in their proper perspective if it killed her.

"He's in the kitchen, still."

She was thinking. "The police have refused to act, I take it."

Brendan nodded.

"Well, the man who is the sort of governor of this part of France, he's called the *secrétaire général* of this *département,* the Alpes-Maritimes, was a very dear friend of your father's."

"Monsieur Thibaud. I remember."

"Yes. He is still in office. If you can arrange for me to use the telephone here for five minutes, I'm pretty sure I can explain things to Vincent Thibaud and he will send people who will take this man away, and no shilly-shallying about it."

"We have to do something," Brendan said, "and we have to do it now. The later it gets the worse it's going to be." He glanced toward the kitchen, where a now thoroughly enraged psychotic lurked.

"I think," said Mrs. Lucas, "you will have to use me . . . as a—what is it?—decoy. I'm the one whom he truly hates. Yes. Do you know what I think I should do, Brendan?" She stood up. "I think I will go now and search his room, very noisily."

They stared at her.

"It's a small room with one of those grilles on the outside of the only window. I have that key to it, the one I used when I straightened it up. When he hears me he will certainly come to interfere with me."

Brendan thought: How like her, *interfere* with her. Only Mother could defuze a butcher-knife-wielding maniac with such a choice of word.

"Then we will somehow contrive to get *me* out and *him* in. That room is like a prison cell. Then," she finished, "I will call Vincent Thibaud and he will be sure to send the proper people to take him into custody. You will remember that name, won't you." She spoke with quiet emphasis. *"Vincent Thibaud."*

To remember in case you are killed, Brendan said to himself in amazement.

"Too dangerous," he said aloud.

"Everything is dangerous here now," she replied.

"Mr. Lucas!" Neville's voice rang out from the door of the kitchen. "Come here!" More peremptory, more Nazi than ever, Neville launched his strongest assault.

Now, Brendan realized in numb terror, he really will try to kill me and all of us. Now he *knows* we personify all those pervasive forces who have dogged him all over the world—those plotters from Princess

Marina of Kent to the most obscure policeman on a Cannes street corner, all bent on depriving him of his property, his liberty, and finally his life. For years (How many? All his life?) he has been consumed with the effort to elude "us," all his emotions burned down to one: to hate and resist "us." And now here we are.

That there had been no trap, no plot against him until his fear created it, was useless to point out to him now; a lifetime of delusions resisted ever facing up to that truth.

"Lucas! Into the kitchen!"

That ringing voice sent Brendan into panic, then settled him into a state of frozen calm.

Mrs. Lucas opened her purse and drew out the set of keys to the house. Briskly she went into the back hall and down to Neville's bedroom door. This she noisily unlocked.

Neville burst out of the kitchen and bolted down the hallway toward her. Xavier and Brendan rushed to head him off. All three converged on the open doorway, Neville in front. Mrs. Lucas had already entered the room. "Neville!" roared Xavier. "A knife in your back!"

Neville whirled to face them, knife cocked; Xavier, knife cocked, confronted him.

An unbelieving expression crept slowly, sickeningly over Neville's broad face. Mrs. Lucas was past him and into the hall. Brendan leaned into the room to grab the doorknob; Neville slashed at him, a painless something moving through his right shoulder; Xavier made a dueler's lunge at Neville's gut and Neville leapt back to avoid it; Brendan had the doorknob and swung the door shut; Mrs. Lucas turned the key in the lock.

They stood panting, disbelieving, overwhelmingly relieved. Mimi and Ariane came up, and everyone examined the long, superficial slice in Brendan's shoulder. It was not bleeding very much. Gradually he began to feel it, a burning and then a throbbing.

While Mimi bandaged the wound, Mrs. Lucas went to the telephone in the pantry and after some minutes obtained the home telephone number of M. Thibaud and got him on the line. She explained the situation to him rapidly. Hanging up, she said, "He is sending some special guards from the Pasteur Hospital in Nice and they will put him in the maximum security ward there and hold him for psychiatric examination." She pinched the skin at the top of the bridge of her nose wearily.

Brendan put an arm around her shoulder, the first time he had ever spontaneously done so in his life. "I'll get you a brandy," he said. "Sit down in the living room."

After he brought it to her they heard a tapping at the end of the hall, then Neville's voice, plaintively: "Mr. Lucas, Mr. Lucas, monsieur, please, let me just talk to you, you alone, come near the door and send the others where they can't hear, please, monsieur."

Ignoring him, Brendan said, "Xavier, you were great." Xavier looked modestly at the floor. Mimi's eyes glowed at him. Even Mrs. Lucas's glance was approving. Ariane beamed.

"You were marvelous, too," Ariane said to Brendan. "And as for Mrs. Lucas—a heroine."

". . . Monsieur, monsieur . . ." went on Neville's voice.

"I'd better see what he has to say," Brendan said. "Stay here." Going into the back corridor, he closed

the door leading to the living room and went up to
Neville's door. "What is it?"

"Monsieur Lucas, why are you locking me in
here?"

"You're sick and you're dangerous. Why am I locking you in there! You came at my mother with a
knife! You—"

"I didn't mean that. She was tampering with my
private things."

She was *tampering* with my *private things!* Well,
Brendan would leave that explanation to the psychia-
trists at the Pasteur Hospital.

"And you slashed me! *That's* why I'm locking—"

"Slashed you!" A foreboding silence, then an echoing voice: "Slashed you. Who . . . what? I never did
anything but . . . I never did that. Slash you? Never.
How could I do that?"

Brendan knew that Neville was an actor, or rather
a changeling in his personalities; passions burst up
and disappeared; reversals of mood were lightning-
like. And yet the bewilderment and distress in his
voice were now so evident that Brendan suspected
he really could not remember slashing him.

"You threatened to kill her and all of us. Listen,
Neville. Some people are coming to take you to a
good hospital in Nice. They'll give you treatment
there, help you to get well."

Silence again. "You're putting me in an institu-
tion," he then cried in a choked voice. "You're help-
ing them to take me in!"

Brendan walked away, back into the living room,
and shut the hall door.

"What's he saying?" asked Mrs. Lucas.

"Same old ravings."

"You know," she said, getting up, "I wonder if there isn't . . . Come with me." She moved swiftly to the end of the room, to the thick oak door leading into the library. Quickly she tried key after key from those on her ring until she found the right one and locked the door. "Just a precaution. Wait."

The library adjoined Neville's room. From there they soon heard a scraping, as if furniture was being moved. Mrs. Lucas took hold of his arm in a cautionary way. There were more indeterminate noises and then someone was moving about in the library; a hand closed on the doorknob and turned it. Then they heard Neville heave a long, slow, despairing sigh. With this door locked, the library was as much a prison cell as his own room.

They moved back into the living room, baffled. "How in the world did he get in there?"

"Well," she said, "just then I remembered that in the wall next to Neville's bed there was a low wooden partition. I saw it when I was making his bed. At the time I thought nothing of it. I supposed there were some fuses or something of that sort inside. And then," sitting down in an armchair she began smoothing her dress over her lap, "just now I suddenly pictured that man, desperate and locked in that room, that cell, and certainly he would search for any possible escape hatch. And I suddenly realized that that panel just might open into the adjoining library. It was large enough for a man to fit through it. Fortunately, the thought occurred to me just a minute before it occurred to Neville."

Mimi gazed at her. "It was pure female intuition,

your getting that thought, and getting it in time."

"Was it?" she said, knitting her brows. "Yes, I suppose you could call it that. Odd, too. Your father said I never had any feminine intuition. He said it was my greatest failing." She examined her lap abstractly. "I rather agreed with him."

And then from the library they heard something like the cry of a cat, a wail. It was the violin. Neville had taken it out of its display case and, though he must never have touched one before, set himself to play on it. The sounds he created were not music but they were expressive, they were poignant in their striving ugliness, they were real, they cried out. Mimi looked at Brendan helplessly; he looked back at her in torn confusion. Neither could say anything to the other. The drama was apparently to end not with a butcher knife in Neville's hand, but with a violin bow.

The knife had not left his possession.

Brendan sat down on the couch beside Xavier, who cocked his lively look at him. "I wonder if they give violin lessons in the Hospital Pasteur."

"He's still got that knife," Brendan said.

"These men coming will have guns."

But they did not have guns. Four young men in the white uniforms of hospital orderlies arrived in an ambulance. They were strong, they looked efficient and experienced, they had handcuffs and a strait jacket, but no weapons. They came in through the kitchen and there Xavier explained to them about Neville's knife. Whether to send for an armed guard was debated, but the orderlies seemed confident and decided they could disarm Neville themselves if he resisted. First Brendan was to go to the library window and try to persuade him to pass the knife through the grille.

He circled the house in the dark, one of the orderlies accompanying him. When they got near the window the orderly hung back out of sight. Brendan knocked at the outside wooden shutter.

"Who is it?" groaned Neville.

"It's me, Brendan Lucas."

"Is it? Is it?"

"Yes, it's me, Neville. Open the shutters, I want to say something to you."

After some delay, the shutters slowly and squeakily parted. The iron grille over the window was still between them. Neville's wide, sallow face stared through the bars; he was already imprisoned. The expression on his face was one of utter despair.

Brendan began unsteadily, "Neville, some men from the Pasteur Hospital in Nice are here. They want to take you there for treatment." He knew that some kind of mortal knell was now sounding deep inside Neville; the fatal toll was reverberating; their trap had closed on him at last. "They will help you with your . . . nerves there. Now I know you don't want to resist going and it would be useless for you to try. I know you have that knife. I saw it in your hand." He looked into the desolate face. "Give it to me. That will show them your good faith, your cooperation. It will help you. Give it to me."

After an interval Neville replied tonelessly, "The knife's back in my room. I don't care about it."

Brendan felt he was telling the truth. Once he found himself locked in, that murderous impulse had once again died away, to be succeeded by apathetic despair, an animalistic search for escape and, fantastically, a bizarre reaching for the violin, the bow: for another life, another self.

Stepping away from the window, Brendan whispered to the orderly. "He's not armed, I'm sure of it. If they go in for him now, they'll find no knife."

The orderly's bright, black, French eyes sucked in everything they could from Brendan's face and voice and then he decided to act. He disappeared around the house.

Brendan swiftly returned to the window. "Uh . . . Neville, I . . . you, the violin, that was something. I wouldn't even know how to hold a violin right. How do you hold it?"

The vacant eyes contemplated him.

"What I mean is, you put the chin thing under your chin, of course, and then you take the bow, but I think it's the angle that counts—the angle you, uh, draw the bow across the strings with, or I mean at, because if you don't get the right angle . . ."

He didn't move nor take his vacant eyes from him.

". . . then I don't guess you make any sound at all or at least not the right sound. I don't know, I think all arts are related and if you have a gift in one, for instance, in cooking, that's an art, God knows, well then, if you're really gifted and you're really accomplished in one art like that, well then, you have a kind of natural way to relate to all the other arts and you understand them instinctively in a way and can do them just the way you did a while ago on the violin. I wonder if you've had any lessons in it." Brendan knew better than to ask him a question; he was incapable of speaking. "Maybe not but there was—"

A noise behind Neville: he spun around, foot thumps sounded and then four big white shapes grabbed at him; spinning again toward Brendan, he battened his hands on the iron grille and pressed desperately against it.

"Denny!" he cried. "Oh, Denny, darling! We could have been so happy together!" His voice broke. "Oh, Denny! If you only knew!" They were prying at his strong fingers, a white arm was around his throat. "You don't know what you're doing! Don't do this!" He went backwards onto the floor.

Brendan sprinted around the side of the house, across the terrace, through the living room to the library door. Neville lay spread-eagled on the floor. "You no more fight?" demanded one of the orderlies in English.

They pulled him to his feet and in a few swift motions had the strait jacket on him. His habitual sallow coloring had disappeared beneath a high, un-natural reddish flush; for an instant Brendan thought he was having a fit or a heart attack. Then in a ringing voice he cried out, "Evil! Evil! You're all evil in this house! This house has turned evil! Thank my God I'm escaping in time!" Somehow captivity and escape had now merged in his mind. "It's all evil here!"

The orderlies held him but made no effort to stop his words. Words, speaking, self-expression: the im-memorial right of everyone, homicidal or not, on French soil. They listened with respect if little com-prehension.

"*Mrs. Lucas!* Your daughter's a slut, a *slut!* Sleep-ing with that man there every night till you came! I

moved him to another room when you turned up.
Okay! Okay! Your son, precious Denny, he, he,
helped them, fixed it up, shoved her into bed with
him. Right! Okay! He encouraged it! See? Your son
and this French guy, they were lovers once, back in
that Holy Roman Catholic college! D'ja know that?
Yuh. One more thing, Mrs. Lucas, one more thing.
Ready! He wants to get in bed with his own sister!
Now tell *me* how rotten *I* am! Do you dare! Now you
know—*that's* why I got crazy, *that's* what happened
to my mind here, all that COR-RUP-TION in the air!
Night and day, everywhere! *Who could stand it!*
See!" He turned his head slowly to one of the orderlies. "I want to go, I want to go," he pleaded. "I want
to go."

Mrs. Lucas, gasping, went up to her room. The
others soon followed, each to his and her separate
bed. Neville had left the house. Now madness is out
of the house, reflected Brendan, and guilt is in it.

CHAPTER
SEVEN

THE NEXT morning Mrs. Lucas was nowhere around when the others assembled in the kitchen. Her belongings, however, were still in her room; she had not precipitously departed for Washington.

After a roll and some coffee Brendan went to the local clinic, where a doctor gave him an anti-tetanus booster and dressed his cut. When he returned to the Mas, his mother was still missing.

"Where could she have gone?" Mimi wondered aloud.

"Almost anywhere," said Brendan.

"In the state she must be in . . ." Mimi frowned and rubbed the calf of her leg.

"There's no knowing," said Brendan.

After a moment Mimi reflected, "It had to be the worst shock of her life—what he said to her."

"Surely she didn't pay any attention to it!" Xavier burst out. "That raving maniac!"

"There's no knowing," said Brendan.

"What kind of mentality would pay attention to that?" Xavier said bitterly. "Is she crazy?"

"Take it easy," said Ariane to him in French.

"The only thing he *didn't* say is that I was sleeping with *you!*" Xavier blurted at her.

"Sometimes," said Brendan from his reverie, "I think Mother *is* a little crazy. If normal is the way most people think and behave, then Mother certainly isn't normal."

"Brendan!" Mimi exploded. "Shut up, don't be stupid! Shut up!"

"You know she believed the part about you and me sleeping together in Denny's house," Xavier said. "You know she did."

Mimi drew a breath through her teeth but remained silent.

"Where could she *be?*" said Ariane. "Should we call th—"

"Police!" Brendan broke in. "The Keystone Cops! They'd be a big help."

"Didn't you," inquired Mimi closely of him, "even *suspect* that Neville was developing some kind of crazy passion for you?"

Brendan stared at her. Then he said slowly, "I don't think it was just for me, me specifically, it was . . . the . . . all of us, the family, the house, the house *party* . . ."

"Because if you had known," went on Mimi resolutely, "you could have saved us all a great deal of trouble."

"How?" asked Ariane.

"By getting him out of here, getting him a job somewhere else."

"A man," observed Ariane, "having a passion for another man doesn't usually turn him into a murderer."

"Denny should have known," Miriam persisted. "It was obtuse of him to have all that emotion loose around the house and not *know* it. Are you sure you didn't?"

Marietta Lucas came up the front steps onto the veranda and into the living room. She looked briefly into the dining room at them.

"Mother," Mimi said, "where have—"

"Where have I been? This is August the fifteenth." She paused. "I see that means nothing to you four Roman Catholics." The last two words were parched with contempt. "This is the Feast of the Assumption. A Holy Day of Obligation. Naturally I have been to Mass."

"We were planning to go this *evening*," murmured Ariane hastily.

Mrs. Lucas pulled off her white gloves. The silence became strained to the limit. It was as though they were in a play, with the next line hers, and she was unable, or unwilling, to deliver it. They could not cue her; they were incapable of improvisation; they sat and they waited.

"I dedicated my Mass," she then said, looking at her hands, "for that deranged man. As you may or may not know, he is a Catholic. I prayed forgiveness

for my lack of charity with him. I see—I believe that
his conscience was an unusually sensitive one." She
spoke more slowly now, standing at right angles to
them. "He could . . . not . . . stand the . . . polluted
atmosphere in this house. The . . . moral . . . pollu-
tion." She moved toward the back hallway. "Nor can
I." She went out and up the stairs to her room.

"Why do we *bother* with her!" said Xavier in a low,
ferocious growl.

"She's my mother!" Mimi cried. "What do you expect me to do!"

Xavier looked indignantly from her to Brendan,
who said quietly, "And she still has some kind of hold
over me."

"I can't," Mimi began to Xavier, "*we* can't have
her believing some of the things he said." She was
close to breaking down. "That you and I slept together—all right, she'll survive that. *We'll* survive
that. But that Denny, that he and I, that there ever
—I have to *know* she doesn't believe anything like
that for a second."

"Not to mention," muttered Brendan, "that you
and I were making it back there in Georgetown."

"She's a Christian, after all," said Ariane, groping
in the French way for the logic in the situation.

Brendan said, "So were the members of the Spanish Inquisition."

"Let's go up and see her," said Mimi energetically
to Brendan.

"I'll come, too," said Xavier.

"No. This is a family affair."

"Am I not in the family!"

"Oh, of course—I mean almost, but I mean this is

a family affair from the past." Mimi tried to make the situation less personal. "What was it Tolstoy said in *Anna Karenina?* 'Happy families are all alike. Each unhappy family is unhappy in its own way.' You wouldn't understand the way we've always been an unhappy family. No one outside could." She kissed him lightly on the cheek. "Come on, Brendan."

They went upstairs.

Mrs. Lucas was sitting in a low armchair in her small, dark, back bedroom. Her half-packed suitcase was on the bed. Her rosary was in her hand. She looked quite unlike herself: drained of energy and purpose and willfulness. Seeing them at the door she straightened in her chair.

"May we come in?" said Mimi. "Or are you saying your rosary?"

Mrs. Lucas drew a breath. "I was just . . . gathering some energy, spiritual energy. It will always save you, no matter what. Come in," she added dryly.

They came in, Brendan shut the door, and they sat down on the bed on either side of the suitcase.

"I don't know why you're packing," Mimi began in a subdued, reasoning tone, "there's nothing—"

"Why is this house polluted?" cut in Brendan impatiently. "Just because Mimi slept here with her fiancé. Everybody does that, now. This isn't 1892!"

Mrs. Lucas clenched a fist around her rosary. "Morals are unviolable and unchangeable. This *is* 1892. And it is 1992 as well. Nothing can change that."

Now *that* is insanity, Brendan said to himself. That is so abnormal as not to be sane. And she is my mother; she brought me up.

"Mother," Mimi said, "even though you condemn,

can't you forgive? We don't want to be married without you, without your approval."

Mrs. Lucas flinched just perceptibly. The rosary
beads moved through her fingers. "Then," she said
very formally, "you would go ahead with this . . .
marriage regardless."

"Yes," answered Mimi in a small voice. It was small
but Brendan heard in it that it was definite. He loved
Mimi for that self-assertion, although he was simul-
taneously troubled by the fact of the marriage.

"Well, then there is nothing further to be said, is
there," said Mrs. Lucas, rising. "I shall be leaving.
Everything I believe in has been violated under this
roof, my own son's roof."

"Not everything," said Brendan. "You don't believe those *other* crazy accusations of Neville's, of
course."

She stared at the floor. "What's to prevent both of
you from flouting *all* moral laws, having so flagrantly
flouted one?"

Brendan felt he had been clubbed over the head.
In a daze of shock he said, *"You're* insane! You.
You're the madness here. More than Neville. You
unleashed it here!"

Shaking, Mrs. Lucas began to move between the
chest of drawers and her suitcase, packing. She
turned to stare opaquely at them, then spoke as
though uncontrollably: "You are not my children!"

"Mother!" cried Mimi piteously. "You're making
the most terrible mistake!"

But Mrs. Lucas seemed possessed as by the proph-
ets of the Old Testament, an essence blindly control-
ling her being. "I don't have children like that!"

Within an hour she was gone, her departure as sudden and complete as her arrival.

And then Mimi discovered that it was not complete. Roaming disconsolately around her mother's abandoned room she opened the closet door. A white summer coat, several cardigan sweaters, a long flowered dress hung there. An old-fashioned flowered hat was on the shelf. A pair of sensible shoes and an old worn pair of pink bedroom mules were on the floor. Mimi wept silently, fingering the gown.

It was a measure of her mother's atavistic emotions as she packed that she could have so uncharacteristically forgotten them.

Later that day there was a call from the maximum security ward of the Pasteur Hospital. A young woman there asked Brendan to bring Neville's identity papers and his toilet things, excluding any razor blades or scissors. She asked him to come at eleven the next morning. Brendan and Mimi then went to Neville's room.

Neville had paid no attention at all to this room. Brendan suspected that except for the time his mother did it the bed had never been made. The sheets had not been changed in some recent weeks. There was a large closet but it was virtually empty. Neville's shirts hung, one on top of the other, eight or ten of them, on a nail in the wall. Shoes were scattered about. The room itself was small and cramped, with one naked bulb in the ceiling providing the only illumination. It would be very difficult to read here. There was a tiny radio but it didn't work. In fact, the room could not in any way be lived in; it could only serve as a bunk for sleeping. And since

Neville had no life outside the Mas Tranquilitat, he had had to try to live, vicariously, with and through them.

There was a battered table with a drawer containing a lot of papers, mostly correspondence. They began to read through them. The correspondence consisted entirely of copies of letters he had typewritten recently applying for jobs as cook or companion or caretaker in various parts of the world—except Canada or the United States—and some negative or inconclusive replies. There was also a sheaf of handwritten verse:

> The stars in the skies
> Begin their story
> At night in your eyes
> So blue with glory
>
> You come from the West
> To land in my nest
> Oh don't fly away
> For life can be gay
> If you'll only stay

There was a sketchbook, with some awkward attempts to draw the Mas Tranquilitat from various angles, together with various views from the Mas. No other subjects were attempted. There was a handkerchief with Brendan's initials on it. There was a snapshot of a sailor, taken on the Croisette in Cannes. There were several holy cards, and there was Neville's missal.

Mimi and Brendan had little to say as they went

through this, searching for Neville's passport and permit to work in France. They were also hoping to find the name and address of a close relative. Brendan had a feeling that they would never find this last.

Eventually they found his Canadian passport. It appeared that his right to stay in France had long expired, and they found no French work permit. Next of kin was listed as Francis V. Thompson, and his relationship to Neville as "guardian."

The next morning Brendan prevailed upon Xavier to go with him to the maximum security ward. They left the house at ten-fifteen, dropping Ariane at Nice Airport for her flight back to Paris, and proceeded toward the hospital.

Speeding along National Route Seven as it sliced through the hills just inland from the coast on this sparkling morning, Brendan took in Xavier's profile obliquely and surreptitiously. He was certainly a handsome man, "chiseled" features and all. Xavier stared calmly before him as he drove along. In that moment Brendan felt great confidence in him: he had so much intelligence that after all he would be a fine husband for Mimi.

"Xavier, that lunge you took at Neville, there in his room, that saved us all."

He made a neutral sound.

"Quite a change," Brendan went on cheerfully, "from when you were—well, cowering in your shower a few hours earlier."

He cleared his throat.

"What happened? You sure did change your attitude . . . found your courage."

"Well," he began in his low-pitched voice, "for one

thing, the son of a bitch killed my dog!"

"Yes, but, my God, before you knew that, he had already threatened to kill *us*, all of us, you, Mimi . . . didn't *that* make more difference?"

He paused, then said somberly, "That was abstract. Titus was real." His voice was a little unsteady as he said the name Titus.

So the unpredictable, and uncontrollable, swings of Xavier's intense emotions had chanced to swing him into bravery and daring just when it was crucially needed. It had been luck, and how much luck would he have in his lifetime, and she with him?

They continued down onto the Promenade des Anglais, the pebbly beach of Nice on their right, the older confections of villas and newer walls of glass apartment buildings on the left, with soaring, spray-topped palm trees lining the avenue.

At the end of it they came into the Place Messina, with its low, solid nineteenth-century buildings, crimson and white, their arcades suggesting an opera set; then inland through the Flower Market, past the fountains and squares of this most appealing of French cities. As the streets began to climb toward the foothills of the Maritime Alps towering massively behind—the Alps, seeming an invincible barrier eternally holding back the North from ever invading here, ever changing all of this, a massive guarantee of the inviolability of the French South—they drew up to a dingy yellow sprawl of barracks-like buildings, the Pasteur Hospital.

They drove through the gate, parked the car in the courtyard, and proceeded past dreary building after building to one at the rear they had been told was the maximum security ward. That could easily be seen. It was two stories high, and all the small windows, inset in thick walls, were heavily barred. In the center of the building was a small archway, and on the right of that a huge door, as though opening on an ancient bank vault or dungeon. There was one tiny grilled window with an inner sliding panel to open or close it. One older and one younger woman, and an elderly couple, waited outside this door. Xavier ascertained that they were to be admitted inside one group at a time. They prepared to wait their turn.

During that wait, Brendan tried to turn his foreboding mind away from this dungeon. He tried, as he always did in moments of stress, to think about the surf breaking on fine white sand, the silver-edged, shiny green wave curling to its climax, and then flinging a frothy cape, lacy and ephemeral, across the pure hard sand . . . the thickness of these old French walls, the stout door which gave one way only: inward. Once inside the maximum security ward who could tell how he might react, what might come over him . . . sand, silver wave, cape . . . with the tension of the past days and weeks, to find himself in this madhouse-dungeon, who knew how his nerves might turn on him? . . . waves sand . . . what if, amid the confined squalor of this place, he started to panic, to yell! Then, the strait jacket, handcuffs, they would have every reason to detain anybody so disturbed.

He glanced at Xavier. He was wearing a polo shirt and tan slacks, and looked abstracted, leaning against the wall.

The tiny panel in the door slid open, an eye contemplated them. Then the great door swung open and a burly orderly admitted the younger and the older woman.

An interminable wait ensued.

Brendan could not get his thoughts back to the beach and the saving freshness of the sea surf.

At long last the two women emerged and the elderly couple went in.

Xavier and Brendan had a desultory conversation about how the Mas Tranquilitat could be run now. Brendan asked about the marriage documents. They were virtually in readiness. Xavier asked Brendan about his autumn plans. Brendan outlined them. The conversation proceeded stiffly. Gradually Brendan perceived that entering this den of madness was going to be just as harrowing for Xavier as it was for himself.

The huge door swung inward and the elderly couple came out. The orderly asked them who they were and they told him. The door shut again.

Then just as it swung inward to admit them, Brendan turned to Xavier and murmured, having to, "Don't let them keep me."

It was an abject thing to say, but it spoke straight from his fears.

They passed into the ward—dull yellow walls, high barred windows. They proceeded behind the orderly down a hallway with rooms opening on both sides. There were about six beds in each room. Some patients, all of them male, lay on beds, sat on chairs or the floor, or drifted up and down the hall. All wore blue pajamas.

In the third room on the right Brendan saw Neville, lying on a bed with his back against the headboard, slumped there, the picture of apathetic, bottomless misery.

If Brendan hadn't been shaken before, he was now.

Neville had not seen them and Xavier had not seen him.

The orderly motioned them to sit down on a small wooden bench in the hall just past the doorway to Neville's room, and there to wait.

They sat and waited. Brendan wondered what would happen if Neville wandered out into the hall. Other patients drifted past, examining them curiously or completely oblivious to them or very suspicious of them. One young man came past ostentatiously exposing his genitals. A great big man roamed up, half of his face swathed in bandages, the rest battered. A little old man asked Xavier for a cigarette, and when he got one asked for two, and when he got two asked for three, and glared murderously when refused that.

Brendan sat completely still and so did Xavier. They did not want to move and they did not want to speak.

Then the orderly summoned them a little further down the hall and into a small office on the right.

A pretty, dark-haired French woman of about thirty sat behind a desk. A small balding blond man in a dark blue suit with vest sat opposite her. She was the doctor in charge of the ward and he was from the Canadian consulate.

Their discussion was brisk and even cheerful. Neville was disturbed and would have to be repatriated to Canada for treatment. A search had already been

initiated to locate next of kin. Brendan gave the doctor Neville's passport with the name and address of
the "guardian" in it, and his toilet things.

Xavier and Brendan, quietly but as firmly as possible, stressed the physical danger Neville threatened
to anyone he identified as his enemy. They empha-
sized that he should be taken from the Riviera under
escort because he had imaginary scores to settle
here, certainly with them and probably with other
imaginary enemies as well. The doctor and the diplomat readily agreed.

It was by now past noon and there was a certain
brisk hurriedness in the air. "Well," said the pretty
doctor, standing up, "one must have lunch, no?"

Everybody smilingly agreed.

Xavier and Brendan started out of her office and
were moving down the hall toward the door, the
orderly behind them, when Brendan saw that Neville was now standing in the doorway of his room,
leaning against the side of it as though too overcome
to stand unaided. Then he saw them. Xavier drew a
quick breath but walked on toward him.

"Monsieur," said Neville in a low but heartfelt
voice, "you've come for me."

"It's all taken care of, Neville," Brendan said ring-
ingly, "everything will be taken care of," and they
passed him and came up to the huge door.

"You've come for me," repeated Neville plaintively, "you've come to take me home."

The poor, poor bastard, Brendan thought. Somebody didn't when they should have, back when,
somebody never did come for him.

It seemed that it took the orderly about five min-

utes to turn the key and remove the bar and chain
and bolts so that the door could be opened; it seemed
that he was deliberately prolonging these simple acts
as a test, a test of their sanity—a final ordeal under
which they would or would not break.

Xavier bridled. Neville began to hover toward
them.

"Get on with it!" said Xavier to the orderly sharply.
"Open that thing!"

The orderly eyed him, and then with deliberation
slipped a final bolt and the great door swung open,
releasing them to freedom.

The sunshine had a primeval brightness that day in
the South of France. They drove back through the
Flower Market—how paint-bright the colors were,
what freshness, what beauty—to the edge of the sea.
There was a small, elegant, open-to-the-sea fish restaurant there and they ordered the greatest fish stew
in the world, bouillabaisse, and a bottle of Pouilly-
Fuissé, and proceeded to regale themselves there in
the soft and caressing breeze from the Mediterranean. They had never felt themselves closer
friends. Brendan's eyes turned often toward a silvery
path the sun made down the middle of the blue sea
toward the horizon, and he knew and thanked God
that if he wanted to he could sail down that silver
path as far as he wished to go, for there were no bars
and no dungeon doors, and all the spaces and seas of
the world were open to him.

CHAPTER
EIGHT

COMING BACK toward the gate of the Mas at
the bottom of the orchard, still in a searching frame
of mind, Brendan suddenly recalled Neville arriving
at the Mas by taxi once and stepping into the brush
near the gate. He had thought at the time, just in
passing, that Neville had dropped something there.
That impression had been completely forgotten from
that moment to this.

He stepped into that clump of underbrush and
began poking around in it with his foot. Xavier asked
what he was doing and he said he was looking for
something. In a minute he had found it: a can of
kerosene, like the ones Neville had bought at the
outdoor market in Cannes that day, empty now . . .

the fires in the hills . . . perhaps . . . possibly . . .

Later they drove into Cannes, Xavier to do some final arrangements for the wedding, Brendan to get his ticket on a Greek Line ship bound, in ten days' time, for Piraeus and his next assignment in the Foreign Service, Athens.

He was going to live in Athens. Maybe he had chosen the right career after all.

Diplomacy: it was not a career to be scorned. What was history except a record of how a people's feelings got out of control, national interests collided, and soldiers took the field and there was a war. Finally one or both sides would lose the early flame in their hearts, would lose land and money and lives; then, at infinitely long last, there would come a moment when those diplomats who had been wrestling with the right words to resolve the conflicts would reword the wording, find the magical right phrasing, and peace would at last fall over everybody. It was not a career to be scorned.

"You're a little *shook!*" observed Xavier as they neared the jammed center of Cannes. "That's why I thought I'd better drive you."

"That maximum security ward," Brendan said. "I can't get it out of my mind. And did you hear what Neville said—'You've come for me' . . ."

"I heard."

"I can't get that out of my mind either."

"You'd better or you might go over the falls yourself."

"Don't be stupid."

They reached the sea front and proceeded along the palm-tree-lined Croisette. Brendan noticed a small group of long-haired teenage boys and girls in their dungarees and leather: hippies. As he stared at them the thought flashed into his mind, They'll be dead tomorrow. "Hippies," he said.

They stopped at the travel agency, Brendan picked up his ticket, and then they made their way slowly back through the crawling traffic and the litter of parked cars all over the curbs and sidewalks to the Boulevard Carnot and up to the Mas.

The next afternoon Xavier, Mimi and Brendan went down once more into the heart of pulsating Cannes to buy some last-minute things for the wedding.

"I'm going to have to get a prescription for sleeping pills," Mimi said in the car. "Xavier snores."

"You don't think you're going to *sleep* when we go to bed, do you?"

"I need eight hours' sleep every night of my life."

They parked the car in Cannes, and Xavier casually handed Mimi his list of eight or ten minor purchases—a certain kind of necktie, a fingernail file and so on. "I'll be over there in the café," he said, and walked off. Her face set, Mimi began his and her shopping.

An hour and a half later when they reconvened at the café they found Xavier three-quarters drunk. *"That's* not the right necktie!" he said scornfully. "Good Christ. Purple! I could only wear that at the ballet, with the other pansies. Go and get me a black and silver one. Narrow."

Miriam sat in her chair, hands folded in her lap, and her Spanish face contemplated him.

"We're all tired and we're going back to the house," Brendan said.

"I'm not tired," said Xavier.

Mimi got up and walked away in the direction of the car. Brendan followed. They waited in it until Xavier eventually slouched into his place. Then they drove back to the Mas, all silent except for long sighs from Xavier. At the house he went straight up to bed.

Mimi and Brendan walked among the orange trees in the heavy heat of late afternoon. "He really is impossible," she said.

"You knew that before."

"Of course, he's not *always* impossible."

"Well—" Brendan began.

"What got into him today?"

"Neville."

"What?"

"Neville. He made Xavier scared for himself, that he might go berserk himself one of these years."

After a silence she said, "That's not very likely, is it."

Brendan took a deep breath. "Neville made me scared for myself too. You only saw a homicidal maniac here. *We* saw the maximum security ward as well. Nobody's perfect. And nobody's completely sane. And that sure does apply to Xavier, and that sure does apply to me."

She shook her head angrily. "Why do I screw up my life with all these *unstable* men. My God, the *ballet* people—"

"Just simple outgoing young athletes, aren't they?" Brendan said, as Xavier might have.

"Mmm. Nijinskys."

"Xavier will sleep it off and be his old charming self at dinner."

She picked an ugly little orange. "Yes, I know.

That's how they drive people mad, did you know that? Alternate pain and pleasure from the same stimulus, the little white mouse steps on the button in the laboratory and gets food, he does it again and gets an electric shock, he dares do it again and gets food and so on until he turns into a blithering idiot of a little white mouse."

"Make you 'shook,' the way he is," Brendan re-flected aloud. "That way he feels he can hold you. I'm sure he doesn't realize this."

Miriam gave her brother a long, contemplating look.

They went out to dinner, to the restaurant in the converted mill, and Xavier, looking his very best, shone with charm and wit and consideration and in-telligence. Mimi ate slowly, deliberately, and didn't say much. When he wasn't looking at her and when she knew he could not see her even in his peripheral vision, her level blue eyes studied him.

Afterwards, they all went to bed early. It must have been about two in the morning, or three, one of those empty hours of predawn when sick people die, that Brendan woke out of some miasma of a dream, some choking nightmare. He recollected only the end of it, his sister rushing down a hallway with her hair on fire, a sheet of flame rising like a bishop's miter from her head, screaming soundlessly, and he holding a hose from which his most furious efforts could not extract a drop of water.

He awoke sweating and desperate. He lay between the sheets and every time he moved the sheets hissed like a snake, or seepage in a sinkhole. He knew where he was but he did not really know who he was.

He moved again. The sheets hissed in warning. Movement was now dangerous. The aching void at the center of his self was now widening, deepening; the human being around it was going to be sucked down into that void and become suffering, nothing more.

He lay in the toils of this waking nightmare for hours or days or minutes or until a kind of comatose unconsciousness closed over him.

The next morning, shaken and fearful, he got up late and was drinking a cup of coffee in the kitchen by himself when the phone rang. He answered it.

"Is that Monsieur Lucas?" an older woman's voice began in French.

"Yes."

"This is the Pasteur Hospital. We are releasing your cook."

"You . . . *what!*"

"We are releasing your cook. He will be leaving in a few minutes."

"But it is not possible! That's impossible! He's insane. He's dangerous. It was agreed that he was going to be repatriated to Canada under escort. You can't release him *here!*"

"I can't discuss that with you. He is calm and nothing appears wrong so we are not going to detain him."

"Has he been examined by a psychiatrist?"

"No, he has not."

"Then how in the name of God can you know that nothing's wrong with him?"

"He has been under observation. He is all right. I

have taken the trouble to notify you and that's all the time I have for you."

"Let me speak to the doctor."

"The doctor's not here."

"Where can I reach her?"

"I don't know. And now that's all the time I have." She hung up.

He slumped against the pantry wall, in shock. He struggled to think clearly, struggled for logic, for reason. What in the world could he do now?

There were three people left in the house. He called Monsieur Thibaud's office. M. Thibaud was on his way to Paris, by car. He called the Canadian consulate. The man he had met at the hospital was unavailable.

He got Mimi and Xavier to join him in the living room. "Of course, the first place he'll come will be here," he said, "to his tormentors."

"Just to get his clothes, maybe," said Mimi.

"Maybe," said Xavier. "Let's see if the local Keystone Cops can be prevailed on to do something this time."

Not trusting the telephone as an instrument of persuasion, Xavier drove to the police station. There was a sign on the front door: CLOSED. OPEN 2 P.M. It seemed incredible but it was true: the police were closed from twelve till two.

There was nothing they could think to do but wait. They had tried every recourse and all had failed: the maximum security ward, M. Thibaud, the Canadians, the French police. They had not taken advantage of the hiatus even to get a gun. They had Xavier's butcher knife, and that was all they had—except that as the cop had pointed out, they each had two arms, against an armed homicidal maniac. There was now nothing further they could do. They waited.

Then Mimi quietly began to cry. Xavier put an arm around her. Sitting down on the other side, so did Brendan. For that moment they all felt very close, one to the other. "Get me out of here," she said tearfully.

That freed the two young men: defense of the castle gave way to damsel in distress; they could leave. Quickly they threw a change of clothes and their toilet articles in a bag and, closing the Mas up tightly, sealing it, hurried through the orchard to the car. Once in it, with the motor started, the specter of Neville lunging from some hiding place began slowly to fade.

"I can't spend a night in that house," said Mimi. "I can't, and I won't let either of you."

"Well," said Brendan, "there's not an empty hotel room at this time in August within a hundred miles, so I guess it's the beach."

Then he remembered the *Ringaling*. Loulou jovially rented it to them overnight at the rock-bottom friends' price.

Brendan knew well how to captain the *Ringaling*, and after supper on the Port of Antibes he decided to pilot the three of them to a cove he knew just below the little town of Théoule. There they would anchor and pass the night. In the morning they would try to figure out what, if anything, they could do to repossess their house in safety; what, if anything, could be done to recapture Neville; who could be found to take responsibility for him so they, so-

ciety, and what was good and hard-working in Neville, could be protected from him. And they might
even figure out how Mrs. Lucas could be reconciled,
mellowed, rendered reasonable, to save her from the
bitter solitude of the old age she was so relentlessly
walling herself into.

But for now there was the evening at sea. Brendan
filled his lungs with sea air as they pitched lightly
along with the receding sun. Against the orangy soil
and cliffs along this westernly strip of coast the flaring
umbrella pines stood out sharply, long sharp shadows
falling beside them. Everything—people, animals
and plants—along this coast seemed to come to attention saluting the decline of the sun.

They dropped anchor in the little cove. Xavier and
Mimi went belowdecks to sleep, but Brendan
dragged a mattress onto the deck to sleep there,
more apart from them. He heard them talking—ar-
guing?—in tense, lowered voices. That night he had
a very confused, sensual dream: underseas, caves,
long-bodied mermaid-like creatures, divers, all swirl-
ing about him, ensnaring him; he must fight, fight,
fight, or else he would drown.

When he woke at the first light of dawn he
shrugged off the dream and whatever its meaning
might have been.

They found some rolls and instant coffee in the
galley, then cruised back through the gleaming innocence of the morning toward the Port of Antibes.

Mimi sat in the seat next to Brendan at the wheel;
Xavier stood nearby. "What are we going to do
now?" she said over the throb of the motor.

"I'll try to reach Monsieur Thibaud again," answered Brendan. "If he can't help—well . . ."

"If he can't help," she finished for him, "then we move *immediately* out of the house!"

"Nowhere else to stay—" began Brendan.

"Then we leave here."

"Where to?" asked Xavier shortly.

"Well," she shifted in her seat, "we . . . I . . . Rome—"

"Rome!"

"The company is in Rome. They wanted me to join them there. They need me for *Giselle.*"

"They *need* you," repeated Xavier incredulously, "for *Giselle!* What are you talking about!"

"Oh listen, Xavier, please, don't let's talk about anything now until we get this Neville business settled."

"This Neville business settled! Screw Neville! What are you talking about! Are you crazy? Why am I here, you, everybody! Why have I spent the summer in and out of bureaucrats' offices getting permission to get married! For my health?"

The quarrel went on all the way to the Port of Antibes.

There they got in the car. Mimi said she would have to take ballet class that day no matter what, which involved going back to the Mas for her practice clothes and dancing shoes.

To try to change the subject she said as they approached the house, "Why do you suppose Neville went off his rocker with *us?* Hadn't he been working for other people around here for years and been all right?"

"I've been thinking about that," said Brendan.

"With those other employees there was always a staff of servants, five or six of them. With us—well, he got control. It became his house. I think now he drove the maid Zinka away deliberately, just so he could have the Mas to himself, control it, control us. It became his house, at last."

"And then," said Xavier with a trace of malice, "maybe there *was* something in the atmosphere around there with us, something . . . compromised . . . ambiguous . . ."

They were silent for a while.

"I'll just get my practice things," Mimi then said a little breathlessly as they drew up next to the gate at the bottom of the orange grove, "and, oh yes, the clothes Mother left—of *course* you're coming in with me."

"Of course," said Xavier quietly. Then he drew his long knife from inside his shirt. "I kept it with me."

For a split instant Miriam thought he might be going to stab her, and then in the next split instant she thought, Well, now *I'm* going crazy!

The three of them walked up through the trees in the sunny morning light. "We'll have lunch at the Festival Restaurant on the Croisette," she said brightly, "after my class." It was important that she establish the reality of their lives beyond this entry into the Mas Tranquilitat.

Brendan unlocked the big front door of the sealed house and they entered into its trapped air.

"Anybody home!" shouted Xavier wildly.

"Shut your bloody mouth!" said Brendan. "Give me that knife."

"Why?"

You're too erratic to have our only weapon, Brendan wanted to reply. Instead he said, "I'm going upstairs with Mimi. You stay here by the door, just in case he *does* arrive while we're in here."

"Good thinking," conceded Xavier.

He's afraid, thought Mimi. What a good excuse Denny has given him.

Miriam and Brendan, listening intensely, hearing nothing but their footfalls on stone and their own breathing, moved together up the front staircase.

They were in the upper hall when Mimi saw bloody clothing at the door of their mother's room. A wailing sound poured from her throat as she sprinted to the door, Brendan just behind her. Here her outcry thickened to a howl of despair: *"Mother came back!"* she screamed. *"For her clothes! He trapped her here!"* Blood was sprayed on the walls and floor and through the ripped wreckage of the coat and sweater, the dress and the hat. In a trance of horror Brendan saw that the blotches of blood went from his mother's room to the dark narrow back stairs. He crept along the hall, and down the steep little stairway. At the bottom the door into the kitchen was shut. He opened it and burst into the room. Neville fell on him, his big arms over Brendan's shoulders. By reflex, Brendan's right hand plunged the knife deep into Neville's stomach. Neville's heavy panting breathing was next to his ear as his body weight dragged them both to the kitchen floor. There was blood everywhere; Neville's knife must be in Brendan's back but he could feel nothing. Neville's arms when they fell were flung back. Blood pulsated from both his wrists. There was no knife.

Then Brendan saw it across the room, abandoned. He lurched to his feet. Mimi stood on the bottom step of the back stairs, one hand convulsively gripping her thigh.

Blood was all over the floor of the kitchen, on the stove, around the sink. It was here in his kitchen that Neville had chosen to bleed to death.

His eyes swam unfocused in his pasty face.

"Mother?" Mimi began shakily. "Mother?"

"Didn't come back. Isn't here. He found . . . he . . . did it to her clothes."

"Who should we call? Doctor?"

"Yeah. Too late. Police."

"Bandage?" she said vaguely. "Tourniquet?"

"Yeah. Too late."

As they fumbled around Neville with kitchen towels and rags, his clouded eyes rolled from one face to the other, to Xavier now standing pale over him. He was the center of all their attention, all their concern, at last. He tried to say something. Sounds came out of his lips with a bubble of blood, but no recognizable word.

By the time the police arrived he had lapsed into a coma, and by the time they got him to the hospital he was dead.

CHAPTER
NINE

BRENDAN wrote to his mother from the Carlton Hotel in Cannes, where he was staying while all the legalisms surrounding Neville's death were exhaustively worked through by French justice. His leave from the Foreign Service had had to be extended.

Dear Mother,

I hope you received my earlier letter about Neville's shocking death. After much thought and much hesitation I am enclosing a copy of a letter from Neville to you. The police found it in your room. You know how deranged he was and this is not intended to upset you but I guess writ-

ing this letter to you was his last wish, and so I'm
sending this copy.

Mimi and Xavier have broken off their engagement, this time for good. As I'm sure you
know she is leaving next week with the ballet for
a tour of the Soviet Union.

> Love,
> Brendan

Neville's letter, which he had scrawled in one of
Brendan's notebooks, spattered with his own blood,
read:

Oh Mother Lucas Mother of Life of the Star
of the Sea Oh Mother the Virgin Blessed of
Life Oh Mother give us this day oh blessed art
thou among women oh pray oh pray us
sinners NOW and at the Hour of OUR
DEATH Oh Mother Blessed art thou among
women and thy Fruit and Thy Womb Thy
Womb Oh Blessed is the Fruit of thy Womb
oh Denny if you knew if you only knew Oh
Family oh Holy Family oh my family oh why
oh never oh never family family oh Holy
Family by Mine be MINE

A week later came the reply:

Dear Brendan—

I have received the copy of that letter left by
that poor suffering soul. He was trying to pray to
the Virgin Mary in it, I think. Still, it was suicide,
and unless he experienced last-minute contri-

tion and spiritual absolution he is in hell.

I note that the engagement of Miriam and the Frenchman is ended. The stain of course endures.

I wish you well.

Marietta Lucas

A few days later Brendan received a letter from Miriam in Rome.

Dearest Denny,

My God it's hot here. And I thought Cannes was hot.

I'm so glad I'm working so hard. No time to think, to see Mother's clothes (that horror will never leave me—I *knew* she had been slaughtered), and his body leaking all over you and the kitchen floor. No time to think about Xavier Farel de Dornay either, poor sweet dear impossible hopeless man. Do you know why I had the affair with him, got engaged to him? To get away from Mother! And, well, once she cut me out of her life for my immoral conduct I didn't need Xavier any more. Isn't that awful! I didn't realize any of this at the time, of course, but once Mother had exited so emphatically from my life, gosh, I felt so free! Free at last, free at last. Dancing! Russia! And one terribly, terribly nervous, selfish, impossible Frenchman on my hands. Please God that he finds some female Job to share his life.

Have they sent you to the Bastille yet? Or to the Maximum Security—no, I'm sorry, isn't

funny at all. I pray for Neville. I think God hears
me—He has forgiven me my adultery, even if
Mother can't.

Love,
Miriam

If Miriam would never forget Neville's leaking
body, Brendan would never forget that the last lunge
at him had been an embrace and not an attack. He
had met the embrace with a butcher knife.

Neville had most feared entrapment, incarcera-
tion, and the very intensity of that fear had brought
it upon him. Brendan had seen that: many people
forced fate to make their worst fears come true.

His mother had most feared being left alone, without family around her.

Xavier had feared losing Miriam.

As he prepared to leave for Greece, as Miriam
prepared to leave for Russia, Brendan sensed that
the two of them were moving ahead in their lives
because they were not clutched by that kind of fear;
they had seen it so closely, a fire storm which had
passed them by.

ABOUT THE AUTHOR

JOHN KNOWLES, born in Fairmont, West Virginia, was educated at Phillips Exeter Academy and Yale University. He worked as a newspaper reporter and then as a magazine editor. His first novel, *A Separate Peace*, received the Faulkner Foundation Prize and the Rosenthal Award of the National Institute of Arts and Letters. Since its publication in 1960, *A Separate Peace* has become one of the most influential books in schools and colleges throughout the country. His third novel, *Indian Summer*, was published in 1966 and was a selection of the Literary Guild. *Phineas*, a collection of short stories, including the one on which *A Separate Peace* was based, was published in 1968, and his fourth novel, *The Paragon*, in 1971.

Mr. Knowles has served as writer-in-residence at Princeton University and at the University of North Carolina, and lectures frequently to university audiences. He makes his home on eastern Long Island and is currently at work on a collection of personal and literary essays.